Finch Books by Ann M. Miller

Single Books
Captured in Paint

I0670710

CAPTURED IN PAINT

ANN M. MILLER

Captured in Paint
ISBN # 978-1-83943-940-7
©Copyright Ann M. Miller 2021
Cover Art by Louisa Maggio ©Copyright January 2021
Interior text design by Claire Siemaszkiewicz
Finch Books

Published in 2021 by Finch Books, United Kingdom.

Finch Books is an imprint of Totally Entwined Group Limited.

CAPTURED IN PAINT

Dedication

To my parents, Keith and Marita.
You will always live in my heart.

Acknowledgements

First and foremost, thank you to Finch Books for believing in this novel. I'm so grateful for the opportunity to share Julia's story with the world. To my editor, Jamie D. Rose, thank you for all your hard work and for being so quick to answer my questions! It's a joy to collaborate with you.

A huge thanks to the entire Shupe clan and all my extended family for their support.

To my best friend, Jennifer Komar, thank you for inspiring me and believing in me. To my Newfoundland bestie, Roxann Butler, thanks for the character names! To my work buddy, Susan Hutchings, thanks for being my confidante.

I wouldn't be where I am today without my amazing critique partners, Amy Bearce and Lauren Alsten. Thank you for all you do. I value your feedback and your friendship.

To my husband, Jason Miller, and my son Logan, thank you for putting up with my endless hours on my laptop and for being there for me through the ups and downs of my journey to publication. I love you both!

And to Jerry and Velvet, thanks for the company and the cuddles.

Chapter One

Luke Mercer's eyes latched onto mine as he strode into history class. I looked down quickly, but I could still feel his gaze. It wasn't like the sympathetic and curious looks my other classmates gave me. At least *they* had the decency to seem embarrassed when I caught them glancing my way. Luke had been watching me with cool disdain, his blue eyes never wavering.

He paused as he passed by my desk. I kept my eyes on my notebook, willing him to sit down.

"Please take your seat, Luke," Ms. Davis said.

He uttered a low, sarcastic laugh and slid into a desk in the next row over.

Luke had transferred from Westdale Collegiate to St. Peter's High for grade twelve, but it was mid-September and he'd only started attending classes two days earlier. People were saying it was because he'd just gotten out of juvie.

I hunched over my notebook, intent on ignoring him. As I doodled with my right hand, the fingers of my left automatically lifted to touch the silver chain that always hung around my neck. My fingertips only grazed bare skin.

Letting out a sharp gasp, I fumbled with my collar, but I still couldn't feel the chain. I dropped my pen and frantically ran both hands over the front of my shirt, hoping my locket had just fallen off and got snagged in the material. It hadn't.

I bent over and searched my backpack. It wasn't there, either.

Somewhere between home and school, I'd lost the locket. How could I not have noticed? It was one of the few things I had left that tied me to my mother, and now it was gone—maybe forever, just like her. As the thought crossed my mind, my chest tightened in a way it never had before, squeezing until I felt like I was going to explode. A lump rose in my throat, and I was struck by the overwhelming urge to cry.

I *never* cried. I'd always been good at keeping my emotions in check. Even in the days and weeks following the fire, I hadn't shed a tear. It was like this wall of numbness surrounded me, keeping me from really feeling.

Now, with the discovery of the missing locket, that wall had come crashing down.

With my heart thumping wildly against my ribcage, I barely noticed when Principal Tobin came on the PA. For a couple of minutes, his voice sounded far away as he read through a list of announcements. But then his tone changed, taking on a sombre note that made me sit up a little straighter. *"And now I have a very important piece of news to cap off today's announcements. As you all know, we lost one of our students this past summer. Nicholas Allen was a bright, motivated young man who was honoured* with a Young Humanitarian Award for his fundraising campaign for victims of the Alberta floods. He also…"

No! I screamed in my head. *Don't talk about him.*

But, of course, Mr. Tobin couldn't hear my silent plea. He kept talking about my dead boyfriend, listing his achievements like a proud father.

Suddenly I couldn't breathe. Something was lodged in my windpipe, cutting off all my air.

"And now," the principal continued, "Nicholas' parents are collaborating with the Red Cross to set up a scholarship fund in his memory. If you would like more information, you can contact…"

I'd known about the scholarship because Mrs. Allen had called to tell me about it before school had started. But I had *not* been expecting to hear about it over the PA today. Hadn't been expecting Nick's name to be boomed out across the school just as I was trying to keep it together in the wake of losing my locket. Talk about a double whammy.

I needed the wall again, needed to build it back up and use it as a buffer against the flood of emotions. But the pieces of that wall lay at my feet, and I didn't know how to put them back together.

I couldn't ignore the images of Nick that popped into my head—tall, lean, handsome Nick with the crooked smile and caramel-brown eyes that could send butterflies skittering through my stomach, even after two years of dating. But I would never see that smile again. He was gone, just like my mother. Just like the locket.

Stop it, I commanded myself, desperate to put an end to the chain of despondent thoughts. *You can beat this.*

My mother had taught me some techniques to use if my emotions started to run rampant—simple things like taking slow, deep breaths, counting to ten or recalling a happy memory…affirmations. I'd never had to use any of them…until now.

I took a series of deep breaths and hoped that I would find my equilibrium.

But the deep sadness and regret only grew, pouring over me in waves as Nick's face floated in my mind's eye.

My face grew warm. The walls of the classroom were closing in on me. I desperately wished I was somewhere else, somewhere I could be alone, where I could breathe in lungfuls of fresh air.

An image of a field of poppies began to take shape in my mind. I didn't have time to wonder where it had come from because a wave of dizziness struck me.

Black spots flitted across my vision, and the classroom began to spin.

I closed my eyes.

"Are you all right, Julia?"

The concerned voice of my history teacher reached me through the dizziness. When I opened my eyes, the spinning sensation stopped as suddenly as it had begun. My racing heart started to slow as I fixed my eyes on Ms. Davis. I took another deep breath, and this time I was able to push back the grief that had nearly consumed me.

"I'm fine, Ms. Davis," I said. My voice was loud and clear, but my hands were shaking. I wasn't sure what was worse—the fact that the layer of numbness had been peeled back, exposing my emotions…or feeling like I was going to faint. What was wrong with me today?

The eyes of my classmates burned into the back of my head. Whispers swirled around me. They were gossiping about the fire, of course, wanting to know more, wondering how I was.

They could wonder all they wanted, though. I wasn't talking about it.

"Quiet, please," Ms. Davis said.

She waited for the whispers to die down then cleared her throat. "Today we're going to start by talking about the St. Peter's Mining Disaster of 1938. Does anyone know what happened?"

"It was a methane gas explosion, right?" Tina Myers answered. "It killed most of the miners."

"That's right. And what was the significance of the disaster?"

"Uh, a lot of people died?" piped up Ron Freeman, the school's track-and-field star. He was swift on the track but not so much in the classroom.

Laughter rang through the room. Ms. Davis sighed. "Other than that, Mr. Freeman. What was the significance of the event in terms of a historical context?"

Emily Saunders shot her hand up.

"Yes, Emily."

"It meant the end of the iron ore industry in St. Peter's."

"Exactly. After that—"

"Actually," Scott Reese cut in, "I think the real significance is that the survivors went nuts."

There was a collective groan from the class.

"Come on, you guys. You all know the stories. They saw some pretty crazy things as they ran out of the mine."

Emily tossed her red hair. "They were probably delusional."

Ron scratched his head thoughtfully. "They were *all* delusional? I don't know, Em. I kinda think the stories might be true."

"Yeah," Scott said with a smirk. "Stories about miners disappearing in a cloud of dust—and not because of the explosion."

"Stories about someone using freaky magic down in the mines!" someone else chimed in.

Ms. Davis held up a hand. "All right, that's enough. Let's stick with the facts, please."

I listened to the exchange without participating. It wasn't like I didn't have anything to say about the mining disaster. After all, my own grandfather—who'd died before I was born—had survived the explosion. And according to Mom, he'd always insisted the rumours about unexplained phenomena were just that—rumours. I could have contributed this information, but the last thing I wanted to do was prolong a debate about death and tragedy. I was dealing with enough of that in my own life.

Still feeling a bit unsteady, I shifted in my seat. As I did so, my elbow struck my pen and knocked it to the floor.

I twisted in my seat to retrieve it, but the girl who sat in the desk behind me had already scooped it up. She handed it to me with a sympathetic smile. I murmured my thanks and was about to turn around.

That's when I noticed Luke watching me from the next row, three desks down. His ice-blue eyes locked onto mine again. *Hi, Julia*, he mouthed.

I frowned at him. He smiled, but his eyes remained cool. I faced forward, anger bubbling in my chest as I focused on my notebook again. Soon the page in front of me was covered with the same line, written over and over in small, neat letters.

Stay in control.

The bell rang, signalling the end of class. I stood, stuffed my notebook in my backpack and hurried from the classroom. In the hallway, I pushed through a throng of students, anxious to get to my locker.

"Jules!" My best friend, Roxy Butler, hurried up and threw her arms around me.

"Hey, Rox." As she gave me a squeeze, some of my tension fell away.

"A bunch of us are going to Tony's for lunch. *Please* say you'll come with."

I shook my head, slinging my backpack over my shoulder. "I can't. I've got some stuff to do."

"Are you sure?" she asked, tucking her curly blonde hair behind her ears. "It'll be fun."

I glanced at Roxy as I turned to my locker. She was slim and petite, but what she lacked in size she made up for in energy and enthusiasm. Since school had begun, she'd been urging me to join a group of our friends at Tony's Pizza Parlour. It had become a Friday ritual of ours over the last couple of years, but more often than not, I said no. No one seemed to know what to say to me, and I couldn't stand being the target of their sympathy.

"I don't think so, Rox. I really don't feel up to it."

Her eyes met mine. She paused. "To be honest, you don't look so good. Are you all right? I heard the scholarship announcement and…" She let her words trail off.

I sighed. "It was just, you know, kind of a jolt to hear his name, but I'm okay." I wasn't okay, though…not by a longshot. After that weird dizzy spell in the classroom, my limbs felt like they weighed a ton, and I could feel the unfamiliar emotions tugging at me again, wanting to get out. But I refused to break down at school. And that meant I couldn't talk about Nick or Mom. "So, are you still going to Scott's party?" I asked quickly.

She nodded. "Are you sure you don't want to go?"

Scott's annual back-to-school bash was always held at the end of September when his parents went on a Caribbean cruise. He'd been having them since grade nine, and I'd never missed one. It was true that I'd told Roxy I didn't want to go. But suddenly the thought of having easy access to alcohol appealed to me — anything to take the edge off. Plus, in Scott's huge house, with loud music and people everywhere, the attention wouldn't be focused on me like it was in a small group.

"Actually, I think I *will* go."

She curved her lips into a bright smile. "Great! We can raid my sister's closet and find you something really cool to wear. And I'll get Jimmy to drive us." She paused, glancing at her watch. "Listen… I gotta go, but you're still coming over tonight, right?"

"It'll be just you and me?"

"Just you and me," she said, squeezing my arm. "Movies, gossip and junk food."

Despite my mood, a smile spread across my face. "Sounds good."

"Awesome. I'll see you then!" She dashed down the hall, and I turned the dial on my combination lock.

When I caught a glimpse of my reflection in the little magnetic mirror that hung on the inside of the door, I gave a little start.

It wasn't the sight of my unkempt hair that surprised me — the thick mass of dark brown was untameable, even on the best of days — but my flushed cheeks and pale lips. And there were dark circles under my eyes that I swore hadn't been there when I'd left for school. Roxy was right. I *did* look awful. I wondered if I was coming down with some kind of flu bug. That might explain the dizzy spell.

I took out the books I'd need for my afternoon classes then shut the locker with a sigh.

And turned to find the new guy staring at me again.

He was leaning against the row of lockers across the hall, his arms crossed as his gaze raked me from head to toe. He clucked his tongue. "It's been a while, Julia Parsons."

"Excuse me?"

"Look at you, all grown up. What are you now, seventeen?"

"Yeah, what's it to you?" I hitched my backpack on my shoulders, heading away from him.

He easily caught up to me and matched my quick pace. "Come on. Is that any way to treat an old friend?"

I stopped and stared at him. "Do I know you?"

"You don't remember me?" His mouth twitched once then stilled. His eyes were bright against his deeply tanned face and shock of jet-black hair. The stubble that dotted his jawline made him look older than a grade-twelve student. "Luke. Luke Mercer."

I shook my head. "Doesn't ring a bell."

"We used to be best buds when we were kids. You and me, we used to run through the sprinkler together? I lived on Ennis Avenue, a few doors down from you."

"I don't remember you living in the neighbourhood," I said, frowning. In fact, I didn't remember any kids living on Ennis before Nick.

"Well, we were only there for a year before Dad moved us across town. I thought I might've made an impression on you, though." He paused, flicking his eyes over me again. "Back then everyone called me Lucas."

Lucas.

A hazy image of a little dark-haired boy holding a ratty teddy bear flashed through my mind, startling me. Where had *that* come from? "When was this?" I asked.

"We were five. Come on. You *really* don't remember us playing together?"

"Not really," I said, my voice high and thin. "I don't remember much of anything from that long ago." My father had died in a car accident that year, and I barely remembered *that*, let alone playing with some random kid who'd briefly lived on my street.

"Anyway, I never forget a name, and your name is flying around this school. When I heard it was your house that burned down on Ennis, I knew you had to be the same Julia Parsons from my old neighbourhood."

I dug my nails into my palms, trying to block out the image of the flames gutting my home. "Yeah. Well, nice seeing you again, but I have to get going."

He held up his hands, palms outward. "Hey, I get it. You don't want to talk about what happened, especially with someone you don't even remember."

"No," I said bluntly, "I don't." I started down the hall, my chest so tight that I was sure my lungs were being squeezed.

He kept pace with me again. "You know what I find ironic? That guy in history mentioning the word 'magic'."

"Oh yeah?" I said, hurrying in the direction of the girls' washroom. The sooner I ditched this creep, the better.

"Yeah. Because that's exactly what I wanted to talk to *you* about." He caught my arm, gripping it so tightly that I was forced to stop. The hard glint in his eyes sent a shiver racing down my spine.

"Let go." I struggled against his iron-like hold, but he didn't budge. I looked around wildly, hoping to appeal to someone else for help, but the hall had emptied as students made their way to the cafeteria for lunch or left to eat off school grounds.

"Don't expect me to believe you don't know what you did to me."

"What the hell are you talking about?"

"Why do you think we moved away?"

"How would I know that?"

Luke leaned close, his breath hot and smelling like cigarettes. "You tried to send me away with some kind of freaky magic. And this past summer, your mom actually did it. Only it wasn't me she sent away. It was my dad. Apparently, you witches can send people anywhere, real or not."

"Okay, you are seriously messed up. How dare you stand there and make up delusional stories about me and my mom?" My face burned. "Now let *go*."

A burst of loud chatter came from the direction of the girls' washroom. Trisha Ford and one of her grade-eleven minions, Kathy something-or-other, stepped out into the corridor.

Luke scowled and released his hold on me. I massaged my arm where his fingers had dug into my skin.

Trisha stopped in mid-sentence when she caught sight of us. Tall and thin, she wore skin-tight leggings and a top that bared one shoulder. A trio of gold bracelets clinked together on her arm as she raised it to smooth down her bottle-blonde hair.

Trisha had been my arch nemesis since grade two, when she'd stolen the doll I'd brought for show-and-tell. Since then, she'd found countless ways to humiliate me, mostly by spreading rumours. I was fairly sure she was behind the malicious stories being circulated about the fire, one of which was the completely bogus rumour that I started the blaze myself. But I'd always been able to remain calm, never letting her see that she got to me. I knew it drove her crazy.

She narrowed her heavily made-up eyes at me before shifting her attention to Luke.

"What are you doing with *her?*"

"Oh, we're old friends." Luke said.

"*Friends?*" Trisha's wide, fuchsia-coated lips curled in derision.

"Yeah, we knew each other when we were kids."

"Wait," I said, looking from one to the other in confusion. "How do *you* guys know each other?"

"We met yesterday. Mr. Tobin asked me to give him a tour of the school. We've gotten very close, very fast." She stepped close to Luke and gave his arm a familiar squeeze.

So, the bitch had found herself a new target. As I stared at Trisha, who was looking all smug now, her arm hooked through Luke's, I thought of all the times she'd tried to steal Nick from me. She hadn't succeeded, of course. Nick and I had practically been joined at the hip. Her ineffective flirtations had never bothered me, but now the very memory of her batting her eyelashes at Nick made me want to scratch her eyes out.

Get it together, Julia. This isn't like you. "Well, that's great. You two are perfect for each other."

Luke extricated himself from Trisha and took a step towards me. I immediately backed away, my hands in the air. "Just stay away from me, you—you creep."

I turned on my heel and half-walked, half-jogged down the hall. Bursting through a side door, I hurried through the sun-dappled parking lot, trying to get as much distance as I could between myself and crazy Luke Mercer.

* * * *

I moved the cloth over the stain, willing it to disappear. But no matter how long or how hard I scrubbed, the stubborn spot remained. I paused to shake out a cramp in my hand, frowning at the culprit on my aunt's granite countertop. It wasn't big—maybe the size of a dime—but it was bright purple and hard to miss. *Stupid grape juice.*

With a sigh, I leaned back over the counter and redoubled my efforts. I barely lifted my head when Aunt Karen came through the backdoor.

"If you're not careful, you'll make a hole in the counter," she said lightly.

"There's this one little spot that…" I trailed off as I caught the smell of pepperoni pizza. Turning, I discovered the source of the heavenly aroma in my aunt's arms. "Well, I guess the spot can wait."

Smiling, she set the pizza on the table. "The house looks immaculate." She glanced at the mop and bucket I'd propped in the corner. "You even did the floors. What brought this on?"

I shrugged. "I had some time." It was more like I'd needed to keep busy or I would've driven myself crazy with thoughts of my missing locket. My stomach twisted. I still couldn't believe I'd lost it. The silver heart hadn't left my sight since Mom had given it to me on my first day of kindergarten. I didn't know of many kids who still had jewellery from their elementary school days, but I'd loved that locket from the minute I'd put it on and had never taken it off. Now my neck felt naked without it. I hoped to God it would turn up in the lost and found at school the next day. So far there was no sign of it there. I'd already called the school office to ask.

"You're home earlier than usual," I said.

As a general surgeon at Grace Memorial Hospital, my aunt worked long days. It was normal for her shifts to last up to fourteen hours. Sometimes she even slept at the hospital.

"Managed to finish at a decent time for once. I thought we'd have an early supper." She lifted the lid on the pizza box. "Thanks for cleaning up, honey. I do appreciate it."

"It's no big deal," I said, taking two cans of Coke from the fridge.

After the day I'd had, doing housework had given me at least a small measure of control. I'd vacuumed, swept and mopped, on a mission to keep my mind off the locket—and Mom and Nick. The grief was threatening to creep in again, and for some reason, I couldn't push it back like I'd been doing all summer.

The encounter with Luke was also weighing on my mind. Obviously, his accusation was some kind of sick joke, but it had rattled me all the same. I bet Trisha was behind it. She could have paid him or something to say all that crap about Mom and I being witches. She *had* seemed genuinely surprised, not to mention pissed off, when she saw Luke standing next to me, but that had probably been part of the act. Mulling the scene over, I pictured her face in my mind, her eyes flashing with disdain.

I'd rather think about Trisha than think about Mom and Nick. Memories of them had been crashing over me like a tidal wave—Mom's lilting voice as she hummed a tune from one of her plays, the scent of her lavender shampoo, the feel of Nick's lips on mine.

It still felt weird, not hearing Mom's confident step around the house or seeing Nick burst through the front door as if he owned the place. He'd lived a few houses down from mine on Ennis, and it had seemed like he'd been at my place more than his own.

I shook my head. So much for *not* thinking about them.

I rustled up napkins, plates and glasses for the Coke and carefully arranged two placemats on the table. I took a bite of pizza, hoping the taste of cheese and pepperoni would mask the lump in my throat.

"How was school?" Aunt Karen asked.

"Fine." I'd already decided not to tell her about the locket. It had originally belonged to my mother, and since the fire, my aunt seemed relieved that I'd continued to wear it—almost reassured, actually. I didn't want to worry her just yet. She probably wouldn't notice it was missing anyway, since I mostly wore it under my shirt.

I took a long sip of Coke. The lump was still there, but it was a little smaller. "They're going over the mining disaster in history again. They really need to get some new material."

Karen gave me a small smile as she wiped her hands on her napkin. "I agree. How are your other classes going?"

"Good." Eager to change the subject, I said, "Hey, did you know they're painting over my mural next week? Jennifer—the contest coordinator—left a message."

St. Peter's held a mural contest every fall. Participants were asked to paint their idea for a winter mural on a piece of stretch canvas while a committee of judges looked on. The winner was given the opportunity to recreate the scene on the large wall that lined the road coming down from Joseph Heights. I had won the past year with my depiction of a snowy village. Now the city was ready to paint it over and give this year's winner a blank canvas.

"Oh, I'm so sorry, honey." She paused. "Is that why you're so distracted tonight?"

I nodded. It was easier to let her think that was the reason. I really wasn't in the mood to talk about everything else that was going on. "Well, that and my artwork for the institute. I don't have much time if I want to send them some new pieces." I had yet to start on my portfolio for the School of the Art Institute of Chicago, one of the colleges I was applying to.

Aunt Karen set down her pizza, concern etched in the fine lines around her mouth and eyes. "Julia, you'll have plenty of time for that. You're doing enough now."

I peered at her over the rim of my glass. She was my mother's sister, but she didn't look or act anything like her. Mom had had unruly dark brown hair like mine. Karen's hair was auburn and styled in a short bob. Mom's face had been strong-boned, with smooth olive skin, full lips and hazel eyes that I couldn't always read. Karen had a narrow face with fair skin, a thin mouth and deep green eyes that always gave away what she was thinking. She'd cried in front of me a few times after the fire, mourning her sister. That was all right for her, but not for me. And it wouldn't have been for Mom, either. She'd been cool and calm, even in the most trying of circumstances. People often joked that I'd inherited her ability to let troubles roll off me like water off a duck's back.

"The more I do, the better off I am," I said.

She reached across the table and squeezed my hand. "I know you think you have to be strong, but just...go easy on yourself, okay?"

I wondered if now was the time she'd tell me it was okay to fall apart, that I didn't have to keep my emotions at bay, that a good cry was healthy, like it had been for her. But she didn't. She hadn't said anything like that at all since the fire. She seemed to understand that I preferred the numbness that shrouded my grief like a cloak.

The problem was that the cloak had suddenly lifted. And I didn't like the feelings that lay underneath.

I didn't like them at all.

* * * *

After supper, I went to Roxy's. My best friend lived several blocks away, but I had turned down Aunt Karen's offer to borrow her car, opting for a walk in the mild September evening. I wanted to be moving, to feel my legs pumping and my heart beating in my chest. The sun filtered through the trees, casting a warm glow on my skin, and a light breeze swept my hair back from my face. By the time I arrived at the Butlers', there was a fine layer of sweat on my body and my face was flushed.

Roxy answered the door and immediately propelled me inside. "Thank God you're here, Jules. I need your math expertise. I'm stuck on a problem."

I let her pull me upstairs. "Sure. Which set are you on?"

"Ah, only the first one," she said, shutting her bedroom door. "God, I hate algebra."

I sat at her desk and pulled her notebook toward me. "Oh yeah. I remember this one."

She propped her hands on her hips. "You finished it already, didn't you?"

"Mm-hmm."

"You freak."

I laughed, searching for a pencil. "Get over here and I'll show you how a freak does it."

I ended up helping her with the rest of the problems. When we'd finished, she flounced on the bed. "I knew there was a reason I kept you around."

I crossed to her dresser and picked up a hairbrush, absently pulling it through my tangles. I could see her reflection in the mirror as she sprawled on the bed behind me, piling her curly blonde hair on top of her head. "It's not like you to do math on a Friday night." I eyed her in the mirror. "What's up?"

She curved her lips up into a sly grin. "Let's just say I'm going to be too busy to do it this weekend. Jimmy's parents are going out of town."

"Oh." I set the hairbrush down and quickly turned toward her desk, straightening her textbooks so I could avoid seeing the anticipation that gleamed in her eyes.

It wasn't so much that I was envious of her relationship with her boyfriend—although I guess a part of me was. It was more that hearing about it was a stark reminder of what I had lost. I'd never have an intimate weekend alone with Nick again. I'd never feel his hands caressing my skin, his movements gentle and tender. His tall, lean body would never again fill the doorway of my house, a mischievous grin playing over his face. His absence—his and Mom's—had left a huge hole in my heart, and it was hard to imagine it would ever be filled in again.

Roxy must have sensed my discomfort because she swore under her breath. "Sorry, Jules. I didn't mean to rub it in your face."

I forced a smile. "You didn't. So," I continued, "something totally crazy happened at my locker after you left today. You know that new guy, Luke?"

"The one who just got out of juvie?"

"Yeah. So, get this. He accused me of being a witch."

Roxy wrinkled her nose. "What? What do you mean, a *witch*?"

I quickly filled her in, finishing with Trish's appearance. "I think she must've put him up to it."

"I wouldn't be surprised," she said, shaking her head. "She probably said she'd sleep with him if he went all crazy on you."

I gave a short, hard laugh. "Probably."

"My God, what a bitch. Why can't she just leave you alone? You've been through enough."

"Yeah, well, she better not be at the party tomorrow."

"If she is and she bothers you, I'll personally kick her ass."

This time my laughter was full of amusement as I tried to picture pint-sized Roxy launching herself at Trisha's six-foot frame. "Now there's something I'd like to see."

She stuck her tongue out at me. "You know, I'm actually really excited for tomorrow night. It's going to be so much better now that you're going!" She sprang from the bed and tackled me in a hug.

"Can't breathe, Rox," I managed.

"What? Oh, sorry." She let me go with a giggle, then dashed to her closet. "I have just the thing for you to wear. Stole it from Debbie's room this afternoon."

"What is it?"

"Her red dress. You're going to love it."

"Oh, I don't need to dress up, Rox. I want to be low-key."

She glanced over her shoulder as she flipped through the hangers. "Are you kidding me? You know everybody dresses up for Scott's annual bash. It's like a tradition. You'll stand out if you *don't* wear something nice. Ah-ha! Here it is."

Seeing the silky halter dress laid out on the bed, I felt a bit of Roxy's excitement rubbing off on me. "It *is* a great dress," I admitted.

"I know, right?" She flashed me a wide smile. "Good thing you and my sister are the same size. Oh, wait! I have the shoes to go with it, too." She ducked back in the closet and stood on her tiptoes to reach a box on the top shelf. "So, what made you change your mind about the party?"

I ran my fingers over the dress. "Honestly? The alcohol."

She turned around, a deep frown creasing her forehead. "Really? You hardly ever drink."

"Well, maybe now's a good time to start."

"Whoa, where is this coming from, Jules?" She set the shoebox aside and came to sit next to me on the bed.

A loud sigh escaped my lips. "I lost Mom's necklace today."

"Oh no. Shit, I'm sorry. I know how much that meant to you. Did you lose it at your house? I can come over and help you look if you want."

I shook my head. "I had it on when I left for school. It must've fallen off somewhere along the way or just as I got inside. I noticed it was gone in history."

"That really sucks, Jules. But maybe someone will find it and turn it in."

I pressed my hands together in my lap to keep them from shaking. "I just can't believe it. How could I have been so stupid? I should've noticed right away."

"It was an accident."

"That was the only thing I had left of her, Rox." The ache was back in my throat again, so painful I could barely swallow.

"It's going to be okay. We can—"

"No, it's not. I'm suddenly missing her and Nick so much that I want to scream or cry or…or drink until I can't feel anything."

"Well, that's understandable. You were probably in shock, and now with the necklace gone, you're just feeling everything all at once." She peered at me with concern. "Even you couldn't hold it in forever."

"It's not fair," I whispered. "Mom should be here, directing her new play. And Nick… Nick should've gotten his award that night."

Roxy rubbed my back. She didn't have to ask what night I meant. "Hey, don't do this to yourself."

I barely heard her. An image of that fateful night burned in my mind. After spending the early part of the evening at an art lecture, I'd gone home to get ready for Nick's ceremony. He had sent me a text saying he was already there with Mom, going over his acceptance speech.

But instead of finding an excited boyfriend at home, I'd found my house engulfed in flames—and Nick and Mom trapped inside.

I'd watched, paralyzed with shock, as the roof collapsed in a wave of dust and debris. The voice of the fire captain, sounding distorted and far-off, told me it was too dangerous for his men to go in. And I descended even deeper into shock, unable to fully comprehend what had happened. I was too numb to feel, too numb to cry.

Now that the numbness had faded, I *could* feel. And what I felt at that moment, sitting on my best friend's bed, was sadness. A deep, dark sorrow wrapped me in a chokehold and refused to let go.

I wished I were dead instead of Mom and Nick.

Roxy shook me gently. "Come on, Jules. I'll take you home. You don't look so good."

"I don't feel good." I tried to take deep breaths, but they came out shallow as my chest heaved with the weight of emotion. If I could have replaced the memory of the fire with a happy one, I would have. But the loss of my locket had brought it all back into sharp focus, and I couldn't fight the emotion that was growing inside me.

The threads of it tugged at me, looking for an escape.

I had to get out of there.

When I lurched to my feet, my gaze was instantly pulled to the poster tacked up next to the mirror. It was a promotional poster that I had designed for Mom's most successful play, *Dragonfly Island*. I'd given it to Roxy as soon as they had been printed. I tried to tear my eyes away, but I couldn't move. I stood rooted to one spot, focused on the image of three whimsical dragonflies set against the backdrop of a white sandy beach curling around an aquamarine ocean.

The room began to spin, just like it had in history class. My vision swam with black dots. I closed my eyes and put my hand out for the bed, reaching forward like a blind man. But the bed wasn't there, and I pitched forward. A sensation of warmth flooded my body like the heat of a noonday sun, and a slight buzzing sounded in my ear. The sharp smell of salt reached my nose. I flailed about, my heart thundering in my chest as the disorientation increased.

Then I discovered I couldn't open my eyes.

Chapter Two

From somewhere in the distance, Roxy called my name. My eyelids remained glued shut. It was like being stuck in the kind of nightmare where you know you're dreaming but your subconscious won't allow you to fully wake up. I was whimpering, still spinning out of control, when a pair of hands gripped my shoulders.

My eyes flew open, suddenly free from whatever force had been keeping them closed.

"Oh my God, Jules, are you okay?" Roxy's own eyes brimmed with concern. She tugged my hand and forced me to sit on the bed.

The room finally stopped moving. "I think so. I've got a wicked headache all of a sudden," I muttered, massaging my temple.

"Do you want some aspirin?"

"No." I shook my head, swallowing hard. "Was just a bit dizzy for a second. I better go."

"Just rest here for a couple of minutes, then I'll take you home."

I didn't argue. We sat side by side in silence. But when Roxy drove me home, she resumed her steady stream of chatter, and I was grateful.

"Are you sure you're okay, Jules?" she asked when she pulled up to Aunt Karen's house. "You looked like you were in a lot of pain."

"I'm okay…just tired."

But I tried not to stagger as I walked to the house, hoping she wouldn't be able to tell just how weak I really was.

* * * *

I stood in the foyer of the house on Ennis Avenue as debris rained down all around me. I opened my mouth to cry out for Mom and Nick, but the sound died in my throat. White-hot waves of fire danced around me, burning my skin, and thick black smoke curled into my lungs, choking me.

A male voice called out from the back of the house, pained and muffled. I stumbled along the rapidly crumbling hallway.

Nick! *My silent scream echoed in my head.* Where are you?

I tripped over something in the hallway, landing on my hands and knees. As I did, the smoke cleared and a dirty teddy bear stared up at me, its hard, black eyes taunting.

I bolted upright in bed, my sweat-soaked pyjamas clinging to my body and my breath coming in sharp gasps.

The glowing red numbers of my alarm clock, showing three-eighteen, were the only light in my room. The rest of it lay shrouded in a darkness that was closing in on me.

Light. I needed light. I fumbled for the lamp switch. It slipped uselessly for a moment between my clammy fingers before I heard the satisfying click. The room was bathed in soft, yellow light.

But the shadows of my nightmare remained.

* * * *

I woke mid-morning and padded downstairs. Aunt Karen had left for a three-day surgery summit. The house was quiet without her, but at least it would buy me some time to see if the necklace turned up at school. I touched the spot on my chest where the heart-shaped pendant used to lay. I felt its absence like a physical ache.

Even though I wasn't hungry, I forced myself to eat a bowl of cornflakes and a piece of toast. The cereal tasted like cardboard and the dry toast stuck in my throat like a wad of cotton. I washed them down with black coffee and grunted, thinking about what had happened in Roxy's bedroom. I was going to need something much, much stronger than Karen's dark Colombian roast. Scott's party could not come soon enough.

Back upstairs, I took a hot shower. As I lathered myself with soap, I shuddered at the memory of the night before. What the hell *was* that? A hallucination? A panic attack? Whatever it had been, it had been more than just a dizzy spell. The sense that I couldn't open my eyes, the desperate feeling of wanting to be somewhere else... The whole thing had been intense and terrifying. Could grief really do that to a person?

The other thing I couldn't make any sense of was the awful nightmare that had plagued my sleep.

It was the first time I'd dreamed of the fire. The disturbing images of flames and smoke had been bad enough, but the *teddy bear*? What was I supposed to make of that? I stepped out of the shower, shivering. My subconscious was seriously screwed up.

In my bedroom, I threw on a hoodie and a pair of jeans with a rip in one knee. There was no way I was going to sit around the house all day, worrying that I might be going crazy. So, without giving myself any more time to think, I grabbed some change for the bus and jogged down to the corner. I got there just in time to catch the Number Two.

I took a seat near the back and stared out of the window as the bus rolled on. I was never fully conscious of the traffic, buildings and trees that drifted by on these trips. Usually I closed my eyes and focused on the sounds the bus made as it lumbered along — the loud hum of its engine, the chime of the bell when someone pulled the cord to request a stop, the squeak of the doors as they opened and shut for passengers. It all had a strange calming effect on me. On the bus, I could be lulled into a false sense of security for a little while. Today I didn't have a destination. I just wanted to kill time.

After about twenty minutes, the bus pulled into a large shopping district. My plan had been to stay on the bus for the entire route and get off when it looped back to Karen's neighbourhood, but the big, newly built Shoppers Drug Mart caught my eye as the bus screeched to a halt. I got off with about a half dozen other people, and a minute later, entered the drugstore through its automatic sliding doors.

Inside, everything with bright and new and shiny. I passed by racks of glossy magazines, prominent displays of school supplies and shelves arranged with colourful bottles of hair products. As I neared the perfumes, a heady mix of scents wafted under my nose.

I skirted the main cosmetics counter and slipped into the makeup aisle.

I hovered over a shelf of lip gloss, trying to choose between three shades of red.

"Julia?"

I turned around. A tube of luscious scarlet slipped from my fingers and clattered to the floor.

Nick's mother, Sarah Allen, stood looking at me from the end of the aisle. Her short ash-blonde curls peeked out from under a green beret. Her thin figure was clad in a long black cardigan. Closing the gap between us, she exclaimed, "I thought that was you!"

"Hi, Mrs. Allen," I said.

She clasped my hand in her own, her expression grave. Dark bags hung under her eyes, contrasting sharply with her pale cheeks.

"It's so good to see you!" She pulled me in for a hug.

When we drew apart, I bent to pick up the lip gloss. "It's good to see you, too. The principal made an announcement about the scholarship fund. I hope you get a good response."

She gave me a watery smile. "Me too. We just wanted a way for his humanitarian work to live on. He did so much for so many people." She paused. "How are you feeling, dear?"

I shrugged, rolling the lip gloss between my thumb and forefinger. *Like I'm going to explode any minute.* "Oh, you know. I'm okay."

"You've always been so strong. I've envied that about you. With Nick gone, I just don't know what to do with myself."

I cleared my throat. "Yeah. Some days it still doesn't seem real."

"No, it doesn't." She dug a notebook from her purse, scribbled something on a page. "This is my new cell phone number. Please call at any time. If you want to come over for a cup of tea or if you want to talk or…anything."

I took the piece of paper. "Thanks. That'd be nice."

She hesitated. "I was actually going to call you today. My cousin works at the fire department, and he heard through the grapevine that the land at your house is going to be cleared."

Something rattled loose inside of me. "What? Why?"

"Well, they *did* close the investigation into the fire."

Recently the lead fire investigator had concluded that the damage was too extensive to pinpoint the cause. I knew that. I didn't like it, but I'd accepted it. At least I thought I had. Now, hearing that the rubble was going to be cleaned up, it seemed so…final.

"You're right," I said in a hoarse voice. "It's just —"

"I know, dear. It's a lot to take in." Mrs. Allen touched my arm. "Listen, Mitch and I would love to see you. I know you must be busy with school, but keep in touch, okay?"

"Sure. I'll, ah, give you a call soon."

"Great." She glanced at her watch. "I hate to run, but I have an appointment to keep. Say hello to your aunt for me, would you?"

"I will." Normally, I would've done the polite thing — asked her if there was anything I could do for her or at least send a greeting to Nick's father. But still shaken by her news, I couldn't find the words.

She patted my arm again. "Take care, Julia."

"You too," I said, swallowing. I watched her walk away, then looked down at the tube of lip gloss still in my hand. Suddenly it seemed like the least important thing in the world. I dropped it back onto the shelf.

I wiped my sweaty palms on my jeans then just stood in the aisle for a moment, thinking about Mrs.

Allen's news. How could they take away what was left of my childhood home? How could they take it away without knowing what caused the fire? It just wasn't *right*.

Somewhere in the back of my mind I knew I was being irrational, but I didn't care. I hurried down the aisle and out of the store.

This time I did have a destination in mind.

With my heart beating like a drum in my head and my throat aching, I stumbled onto the bus that would take me to Ennis Avenue.

* * * *

A short time later, I stood in front of the pile of rubble that used to be my home.

My legs were frozen in place. I stared at the mass of debris where the two-storey once stood. Scorched wood, broken glass and scraps of metal were strewn across the square of land that would soon be cleared.

Before today, I'd avoided my old neighbourhood at all costs. But after running into Nick's mother, the burning need to view the damage firsthand had reared up and taken me by the throat. It wasn't like I could figure out the cause of the fire just by looking at it. I just wanted to—I don't know—try to make some sense out of that night. It seemed like I'd been living under a rock the last two months, sitting idly by and accepting what everyone told me without batting an eyelash.

Now a million questions zoomed through my head, and I wanted answers. How had the fire spread so quickly? Why hadn't Mom and Nick been able to get out in time? We had smoke detectors. And the biggest one of all... What had caused it in the first place?

The fire department needed to try harder. They shouldn't stop until they found out who or what was responsible for burning down my home. That fire had taken everything from me. *Everything.*

The piles of wood and debris swam in front of my eyes. I backed up against a tree and brought my hand to my face. Was I...crying? Furious, I wiped away the tears before they had a chance to fall.

I shook my head and sucked in a breath. And that's when my gaze fell on the JP plus NA etched into the ground. Two years ago, when they'd been putting in a new sidewalk, Nick had used a stick to draw our initials in the fresh cement mixture. I sighed, falling to my knees to run my fingers over the letters. Two years ago, he'd become my boyfriend, but we'd been friends for a long time before that.

I closed my eyes and relived that summer day when we'd met for the first time. I'd been riding my bike when a rut in the sidewalk had caused me to topple over. Suddenly a dark-haired boy had been by my side, asking if I was okay and offering up a bag of M&Ms to take my mind off my skinned knees. From that moment on, we had been the best of friends. Over the years, we'd been there for each other through thick and thin, through the highs and lows of growing up. And no one had been prouder than me when, at the age of seventeen, Nick was recognised by the Canadian Red Cross. He would receive a Young Humanitarian Award at a dinner in July, eleven years after we'd met.

Of course, he never got that award. The fire had robbed him of that chance...had robbed him of his life.

My throat started to swell again. Why had I come here? Why was I torturing myself? I had to go, had to get away from this street and all the memories. But I was feeling dizzy and all I wanted to do was keep my eyes closed.

Stay in control.

The mantra in my head, coupled with the sound of a nearby car door slamming, brought me back. I surged to my feet, dashed out of the yard and ran from Ennis Avenue as fast as I could.

* * * *

I was glad to have the house to myself while getting ready for the party. With the borrowed dress and shoes on, I stood staring into the mirror that hung in the front hallway. The halter dress was made out of a silky fabric that clung to my hips and had a hem that fell mid-thigh. I slipped on a jean jacket to cover my bare arms and shoulders and pursed my lips in the mirror. They were coated with the rosy red lipstick I'd borrowed from Aunt Karen. I tried a smile. It looked totally fake.

The forced smile turned to a scowl as I caught sight of my unruly hair tumbling down my shoulders. I twisted the whole thing into a knot at the nape of my neck and secured it with a clip, just as Jimmy's horn sounded outside.

Roxy and Jimmy greeted me cheerfully as I slid into the backseat.

"Hey, guys."

Jimmy glanced at me before pulling away from the curb. "So cool that you decided to come out tonight, Jules. Rox was beyond stoked. I mean, I literally had to put the phone down and back away from it. She was screeching that loudly in my ear." He put a hand to it now, wincing. "I don't think my hearing will ever be the same."

When I smiled this time, it did feel genuine. I hadn't realised how much I'd missed lanky, goofy Jimmy. "Well, I couldn't miss the party of the year, could I?"

"Yeah, should be a good time," Jimmy said. "And a bunch of us are going to the football game next Friday, maybe get a bite to eat after. You should come."

"Uh, maybe." The truth was that I was far from ready to plunge back into social events. I was just going to the party because of the alcohol. It would be flowing freely there, and I planned on consuming as much as it took to take the edge off.

My gaze flicked over the empty seat beside me, the seat where Nick would sit when we went on double dates. I stared straight ahead for the rest of the ride, my chest tight.

We arrived at Scott's house just as people were starting to trickle inside. I stepped into the foyer behind Roxy and Jimmy, blinking up at a huge crystal chandelier that glittered from the ten-foot ceiling.

Even though I'd been to parties at Scott's before, I was still blown away by the place. The house was like a mansion. It had plush carpeting, gilt-framed mirrors and crown moulding. There was a big-screen TV in every room, a Jacuzzi, sauna, swimming pool, pool table, walk-in closets and a guest loft above a double-car garage that had its own private entrance. Couples often escaped to the loft for their own little private party.

We headed to the kitchen for a drink. At the long stainless-steel island, Roxy and I mixed vodka and cranberry juice, while Jimmy grabbed a beer and joined a group of his friends from the lacrosse team.

Leaning against the counter, I took a long swallow of my drink. It burned my throat and sent a trail of warmth down my stomach. I sighed. That was what I needed.

I listened to Roxy's chatter with half an ear as I continued to drink. By the time my glass was empty, I was already feeling steadier, the emotions pushed down beneath the surface where they belonged. I poured another drink and gulped it down. Oh yeah, I had a good buzz going now. I was lighter, the constricted feeling in my chest considerably loosened. I even felt my face break into a bright smile as a few girls from our grade swarmed around us, begging us to join them in a game of pool downstairs in the rec room.

"I'm in!" Rox said. "What about you, Jules?"

"Maybe in a little bit. I want to check out the patio first."

"All right. But don't be too long." She leaned towards me and, in a conspiratorial whisper, said, "I need your help kicking their asses." Then she bumped her hip against mine with a laugh. Obviously, I wasn't the only one enjoying a nice buzz.

I gave her a playful shove. "Go on. I'll see you soon."

In order to get to the back patio, I would have to go through the living room. With a new drink in hand, I headed in that direction, eager for some fresh air.

In the cavernous living room, with its large ornate fireplace and long leather sofas, Trisha sat with one of her cheerleader friends.

Emboldened, I walked over to them, my steps just a tad wobbly. "Hey, Trisha."

Trisha raised her head, her eyes narrowed. She was wearing *way* too much makeup. The thick eyeliner, bright blush and heavily caked-on fuchsia lipstick made her look even trashier than usual. Her purple miniskirt was way too tight and the matching top way too low. If she leaned forward even a little, her boobs would probably fall out.

"What do you want?" she said.

"Nothing," I murmured. "I'm just surprised you aren't here with Luke, since you guys are *so* close."

Trisha scowled. "He was supposed to meet me here, but he didn't show. Not that it's any of your business."

"He blew you off, huh? Tough break."

She tossed her hair over her shoulder. "Whatever." Turning back to her friend, she bent her head and whispered something in her ear. The other girl laughed in response.

I rolled my eyes and took another drink. "I know you asked Luke to call me a witch. And I also want you to know I don't care. Don't you get it by now?" I added, swaying on my feet a little. "Your pranks don't bother me, especially this stupid one."

Trisha rounded on me. "What prank?"

I set my empty glass down on the mantel. "Don't play dumb with me. You got Luke to make up some crazy story about me doing witchcraft on him when we were kids. I mean, really, Trisha? Witchcraft? That's a new one, even for you." Through the haze of alcohol, the notion struck me as being not only crazy but completely hilarious. A laugh bubbled up in my chest.

Trisha's face contorted into a look of utter contempt. "I don't know what you're talking about, but you better get out of my face before I get *really* pissed off."

"You can deny it all you want," I said, still laughing. "It's obvious you put him up to it. You've given sexual favours for a lot less."

Trisha's jaw dropped and her face went an even brighter pink. "You...you little bitch!"

"Anyway, have fun being stood up." I waggled my fingers at her and strode from the room. Out in the front hallway, I stopped and leaned against the wall, shaking my head in wonderment. I couldn't believe I'd finally stood up to Trisha. It was amazing what a little liquid courage could do.

Now, where was I heading? Oh right, the patio. The confrontation with Trisha had distracted me so much that I'd gone in the wrong direction.

A group of girls entered the foyer, their loud voices carrying around the corner.

"Did you guys see Julia Parsons at school this week?" one of the girls asked. "Ugh, she's still going about her day like nothing happened."

"I know," another voice chimed in. "I heard she didn't show *any* emotion at the funeral. How heartless is that?"

"Yeah, they're calling her 'Ice Princess'. Sounds about right."

"I would totally lose it if my mom and boyfriend died."

They rounded the corner and stopped in their tracks when they saw me. Their chatter ceased abruptly. In the awkward silence, I lifted my chin and studied each one of their mortified faces in turn. *Tenth graders.*

"Hi, girls," I said in a cool voice. "Well, don't look so surprised to see me. Just going about my business." Anger penetrated my buzz, coursing through me in thick, hot waves. My hands started to shake. Just like that, I was losing control of my emotions again. I needed more alcohol to beat them back.

Pushing past the girls, I hurried to the kitchen and grabbed a half-empty bottle of vodka from the counter. A couple of football players whistled and hurled catcalls at me, but I ignored them and ran from the room.

Back in the hallway, I hesitated, the girls' words resounding in my head. I wouldn't have been able to show any emotion at the funeral, no matter how much I'd wanted to. At that point, the shock of Mom's and Nick's deaths had still been wrapped around me like a cocoon. I couldn't think, couldn't feel. Everything and everyone had moved around me in a blur.

Now I wished for that numb-like state again. All I wanted to do was drink until I couldn't feel anymore.

I looked around wildly, anxious to find somewhere to be alone. The problem was that there was nowhere to *be* alone at this party. The rooms were crammed with people drinking or making out. Music reverberated through the house, and the roar of laughter and conversation made my head hurt.

Then I remembered the guest loft.

While I might not be totally alone—a few people might've already gravitated up there—it would definitely be quieter than the main house.

Clasping the bottle against my chest, I shouldered my way through a new crowd forming in the foyer and stumbled onto the front steps. I paused for a moment to draw in several breaths of the cool, crisp air, then hurried around the side of the house.

The loft was situated over the three-car garage. I mounted a short flight of stairs and turned the knob on the solid oak door. Finding it unlocked, I pushed it open and looked around.

The large, open space had a combination living-dining area with white Persian rugs, glass tables and brocaded lamps. An adjacent kitchenette gave way to a short hallway that led to the bedrooms and bathroom. I heard a giggle from one behind one of the closed doors, but the main part of the loft was empty. That was good enough for me.

Heaving a sigh of relief, I sank onto a plush brown sectional and curled my legs underneath me. I tilted the bottle up to my mouth, took a long swallow, then coughed and sputtered as the vodka stung my throat.

"God, that's nasty by itself," I muttered. Still, I forced myself to take a second drink before plunking the bottle down on the coffee table with an unsteady hand. With my eyes closed, I leaned back against the sofa and let the alcohol do its work, numbing my pain like ice on a swollen, throbbing ankle. Soon a sleepy, relaxed feeling flowed from my head to my toes.

Through my mellowed state, I heard the door to the loft open and close. I opened my eyes, lifted my head and gave a slight jerk of surprise. Luke stood across the room.

Perfect. Just perfect.

He wore tattered Levi jeans and a black T-shirt emblazoned with the gold and white Harley Davidson logo. His jet-black hair stood up in wild tufts, and a cigarette was stuck behind one ear. He stared at me with eyes that glittered like blue ice, his dark brows raised slightly.

"So this is what a witch does on a Saturday night — hides out at a party, drinking alone."

"If Trisha asked you to follow me and continue your little witchcraft story, you can forget it. I already told her I figured out her sick joke."

"A joke," he repeated, his voice flat.

I snorted. "Come on. Enough is enough already. She's had her fun. Now just leave me alone, okay?"

He dug in his jeans pocket and withdrew a silver lighter. Then he crossed to the sectional and sat down close beside me. He plucked the cigarette from behind his ear, and as he lit it, I noticed the initials LM engraved on the front of the lighter in big block letters. He took a long drag before speaking again.

"Cut the bullshit, Julia, and just admit what you did."

"Me? What did *I* do? Trisha is the one who—"

"Would you shut the hell up about Trisha? This has got nothing to do with her."

"But she said you were supposed to meet her here and—"

"She lied," he said, his tone rife with fury. "I only came to this lame party because I heard you tell your friend you were coming."

"No, you're the liar. You're new at school and Trisha pounced on you. She made you say those things."

"She didn't make me say or do anything. Look... I heard the rumour around school. She wanted your boyfriend. You can blame her all you want for that, but—and I repeat—she has nothing to do with *this*."

Through the fog of alcohol, a sense of apprehension was beginning to creep in, but I fought to keep my voice calm. "Just because Trisha didn't tell you to say it doesn't mean you're not lying. And I don't have to sit here and listen to you. You're...you're just some psycho who just got out of juvie."

"Oh, juvie." He laughed humourlessly. "That was just a misunderstanding. Some asshole store owner charged me for robbery. Truth was, I was just an innocent bystander. But enough about me." He tossed his half-smoked cigarette onto the snow-white carpet and ground it under his shoe. His mouth turned up in a nasty smile. "Let's talk about you—and what you did to me when we were kids."

"I didn't do *anything* to you." He was taking this way too far, and I wasn't going to stay and listen to his delusions. I lurched to my feet. "I have to go."

I had barely taken a step when Luke shot up and seized my wrist. He yanked me back onto the sofa. I let out a cry of indignation and struggled to stand up again, but he tightened his grip on my wrist, holding me in place.

"It seems like I need to refresh your memory, Parsons."

My stomach twisted into anxious knots, but I forced myself to take a deep breath. "I told you that I don't remember anything from when I was five."

"Well, I don't remember a lot either. My father does, though. He saw everything that happened that day."

"*What* day? You're not making any sense." And he was a total psycho. I was regretting my decision to come up to the loft alone.

The cool blue eyes locked with mine, boring into me with an intensity that unnerved me. "The day you threw a temper tantrum and used your freaky power. You opened up some world and I almost got sucked into it. You tried to send me away, witch. And a couple months ago, your mom used the same magic on my old man. Only she succeeded."

Opened up a world? The idea was so ludicrous I almost laughed. I would have if he hadn't been holding me against my will. "That's crazy. Absolutely crazy."

He cocked an eyebrow. "Is it?"

"Yes," I said through clenched teeth. "Now let me go."

"I'm not letting you go anywhere until you bring my father back."

By now my mellowed state had completely faded. It its place was a hot rush of anger that had me reeling. "I don't know what you're talking about, but I'm sick of your twisted games. Now take your hand off me. My friends are waiting for me downstairs."

In response, Luke pressed his fingers into my flesh so hard that I yelped in pain. "This isn't a game. This is my dad's life we're talking about. Now, get him back."

"And where exactly do you think he is?"

"Your mother sent my dad into that ugly mural you painted." He leaned close, and the scent of cigarettes irritated my nostrils. "Like I told you yesterday, you Parsons witches can send people anywhere you want — even into a goddamn painting."

My anger rose even higher now, and I was breathing rapidly as I tried to contain it. My face burned and my head ached. "Stop it," I said, my voice a hoarse whisper. "Stop it right now."

But even as I said it, I recalled what had happened with the poster in Roxy's room — that freaky sensation of not being in control of my body — and the recent dizzy spells. Then, like a bolt of lightning, an image of the ratty teddy bear flashed through my brain again. Except this time, it hovered in the air, suspended against a backdrop of blue and white. I swallowed and shook the image from my head.

"You know it's true," Luke said. "Now I need you to do whatever it is you do when you move people between worlds and get him out of there."

Before I could say anything else, the door to the loft opened and Roxy and Jimmy burst in.

Jimmy took one look at Luke's hold on me and rushed forward. "Hey, let her go!"

Luke grunted but released me, lifting his hands up in surrender. "No worries, man. We were just having a little chat."

"It didn't look like that to me." Jimmy narrowed his eyes at Luke.

"Chill out," Luke said. "This has got nothing to do with you."

"Actually, it does," Roxy said. "Julia's our friend." She turned to me. "Are you okay? Did he hurt you?"

I took another deep breath, and as I focused on my best friend, my vision cleared. I found my centre again. "No, I'm all right," I answered her, rubbing my wrist.

"When you didn't come downstairs, I started to get worried. Someone told me they saw you come up here."

"Yeah, I just wanted a few minutes alone. Then this creep" — I nodded in Luke's direction — "followed me up here. But I'm fine, really. I just want to go home."

"You got it," Jimmy said, still shooting daggers Luke's way. "Don't let me see you touch her again."

Luke ignored him. "We're not done here, Julia."

"What's he talking about?" Roxy asked.

"Nothing. He's crazy. Let's go."

We moved to leave. Jimmy led the way, Roxy bringing up the rear. At the entrance to the loft, I couldn't help glancing over her shoulder. I immediately wished I hadn't. Luke's eyes were cold, dark and calculating. I could feel them on me even as I turned and walked out of the door.

Chapter Three

The sun slanted in through my half-open blinds. Wincing at the bright light, I rubbed my temples and eased myself to a sitting position in bed. A wave of nausea rolled through my stomach as the events of the night before came back to me.

I swung my legs over the side of my bed, tucking my tousled hair behind my ears. Then, pushing myself up, I shuffled over to the window and snapped the blinds all the way closed. I heaved a deep sigh as the harsh light was muted.

After Jimmy and Roxy had rescued me, we'd left the party. On the drive home, they'd wanted to know what had happened with Luke, of course. I'd told them it was all part of Trisha's weird game, but I didn't miss the worried look that passed between them. They'd both known me for a long time. They knew when I wasn't telling the whole truth and both of them had been ready to kick Luke's ass. I'd assured them that I was okay and had every intention of steering clear of him. Finally, they'd dropped it, but I could tell they weren't going to let it go. It had been a relief to be alone again in my room.

I'd had a restless night, replaying my warped conversation with Luke over and over again. His insistence that I'd performed some sort of witchcraft on him when we had been kids was insane, as was his story about Mom sending his father into a painting—*my* painting. It was beyond crazy. But his voice kept echoing in my head.

'You Parsons witches can send people anywhere you want.'

My hands trembled slightly as I pulled my hair back in a ponytail. He was mad, a psycho just out of juvie. And yet, as I pulled on jeans and a sweater, I felt a flicker of uncertainty. Maybe he *was* deranged, but I couldn't deny the dizzy spells I'd experienced lately—dizzy spells that came over me when I couldn't control my emotions. There was a strange pull that came with those dark emotions, the pull of wanting to be somewhere else. A grief like I had never known was taking over at unexpected moments. It was getting harder and harder to find my equilibrium.

I lay back down on my bed. I didn't know what was real anymore, and I didn't want to think about Luke or the dizzy spells. If I could get back to sleep, I could shut off my brain. Turning onto my side, I closed my eyes and willed myself to fall asleep. But I kept seeing the teddy bear in my mind, floating against that blue-and-white background that I could only assume was the sky.

What did it mean? Why did that specific image stand out sharply in my mind?

I opened my eyes, my gaze wandering. It fell on the bookshelf across from my bed. A thick photo album was wedged onto the bottom shelf—one of Mom's old albums. Because she'd left it at Aunt Karen's one day, it hadn't been destroyed in the fire with all the others.

I hadn't looked at it in a long time, but I knew there were some early photographs of me and Nick in there. If I had really played with Luke as a kid, maybe Mom or Dad had snapped a picture of him. They'd taken photos of everything when I was growing up.

Before I knew what I was doing, I'd slid the album out and laid it on the bed. I paused with my hand on the cover. Did I really want the memories of Mom and Nick coming back again? I needed to forget how happy my life had once been. It only caused me pain to relive it, and the last thing I needed was to have feelings clouding my judgement, making the world a blurry place. But I was too curious to see if Luke was in the album. I just needed a quick look. Maybe something would jog my memory.

I flipped through the first several pages. There were old photos that had captured me first as a baby, then as a toddler. Dad had taken most of those early ones, so Mom was with me in a great many of the shots. I couldn't help pausing at one in particular when I was about two. Mom was holding me in her lap, and we wore identical smiles. It sent a pang through my heart. Everyone always said how much I looked like her, with our dark hair and olive skin. Everyone commented on how much alike we were — neat, organized, calm and steady.

There weren't any pictures of Luke, but there were several of Nick, starting when he'd moved onto Ennis Avenue. I'd meant to put the album away if Luke wasn't in it, but as I turned the pages and saw me and Nick grow up through the pictures, I couldn't stop. I couldn't tear my eyes away from the tall boy with the crooked smile and caramel-brown eyes—the caring, strong-willed boy who I had loved with all my heart.

A lump lodged in my throat like a rock. I closed the album with a snap. When I got up to return it to the shelf, a loose photo fell from between the pages and fluttered to the floor. I picked it up. My eyes locked onto an image of me, Mom and Nick standing in front of the house on Ennis Avenue.

It had been taken the day of our junior high graduation, a moment snapped by a neighbour. We posed on the front walkway, smiling happily. Nick stood behind me, his hands resting on my shoulders. He had on a grey suit and burgundy tie while I wore a white cotton dress and a silk scarf. Mom stood to one side of me, leaning in close, her arm around Nick. The June twilight swirled around us in shades of deep lavender and burnished gold. The branches of the maple tree that overhung the walk curled over our heads, fragrant green leaves sprouting from its dangling fingers. The house rose up behind us, its grand peaks partially obscured by the lengthening shadows, its coat of butter yellow still shining in the circle of the setting sun. Lights winked from the windows, warm and inviting.

After the graduation ceremony, Nick's parents had hosted a party for us at their house. I didn't remember much about the party itself. In my mind, it was overshadowed by those fleeting moments at the end of the night, when he'd walked me home and kissed me for the first time.

Since he lived just down the street from me, it had been a short walk from his house to mine. But we'd lingered on the sidewalk in the breezy June air, chatting about the graduation and making plans for the summer ahead. When he put his hand in mine, my stomach turned topsy-turvy. Then, when we stopped at my front door, he leaned over and pressed his lips to mine, catching me by surprise. The kiss was brief, but soft and warm, and sent my heart into overdrive. When he pulled back, he looked at me as if I were the only person in the world.

I'd stepped into the house that night feeling as though I was walking on air.

Now I put a hand to my lips. There'd been at least a hundred more moments like that, stolen kisses on the street where we'd grown up together.

I set down the album, my eyes still on the picture. All I had now were memories.

I straightened, alarmed to find that my eyes were damp again. I slipped the photo back in the album and slammed it shut.

But it was already too late.

The tears began to flow freely down my face and shuddering sobs racked my body as the dam burst. My centre was utterly and completely gone. Everything I'd been holding back poured out of me. I cried for all I had lost, for the unfairness of it all. I cried because I was angry, because I was sad and because I was afraid.

Again, I was struck by the burning need to escape everything.

Wisps of black danced across my vision. My head ached, and my sobs were cut off as I let out a cry of pain. I closed my eyes against the dizzying sensation. As soon as I did, they were sealed shut. I tried to open them again, but they wouldn't budge. All I could see was the darkness of my eyelids, writhing with spots of orange. I remained in that blind state for what seemed like forever.

Then a fresh breeze caressed my face and ruffled my hair. The smell of fragrant grass reached my nostrils.

Finally, I was able to open my eyes. I gasped.

In the spot where my bed should have been was a doorway, only it wasn't a real doorway with a wooden frame. It was more like a shimmering rectangle that floated in front of me, a rectangle that was awash with swirling colour — pale blue, rich greens and vivid red. It was a palette so bright that it made my eyes burn, but I couldn't tear my gaze away.

The colours shifted, became more defined, and I realized I was looking at a field crammed with flowers. I barely had time to process this, though, because the breeze I'd felt against my skin had morphed into a wind so strong that it took my breath away, a wind that originated from the iridescent bubble that hovered in my room.

It whirled around me in a vortex, sweeping me off my feet. I didn't even have time to scream before it pulled me into the bubble.

This time, I squeezed my eyes shut on purpose. For a moment, I was suspended in mid-air, my arms and legs flailing wildly. Then I landed knee deep in a field cushioned with soft, velvety…poppies?

I was dreaming. I had to be. This could *not* be real. I ran my hand through the bright red flowers. They definitely felt real, as did the lush patches of grass waving in the wind. I staggered to my feet. Just beyond the poppy blooms, rows of tall, thin trees danced against a glistening blue sky. And in the distance a series of hills stretched out, coated in forest green.

I spun around as I took it all in, my heart doing a mad dance in my chest. The colours were so vibrant that they were almost blinding. The wide expanse of field and the surrounding scenery were dazzlingly real and achingly familiar.

It couldn't be, could it? It just wasn't possible.

A sense of panic and fear seized me by the throat.

I fell to my knees again as fresh tears seeped from my eyes and streamed down my face. "Please let this be a dream. Please. I want to be home."

Another bubble opened directly in front of me, this one a blur of lavender and cream. Suddenly I was sailing through the air again, pulled out of the world of the poppy field by the same invisible force that had carried me into it.

I struck my bedroom floor with a thud. I raised my head slowly, my breath coming in sharp gasps. My hands shook as I pushed my tangled hair out of my eyes. I wiped my cheeks and waited for my breathing to slow. When it did, I got to my feet and glanced around the room.

The bubble was gone.

I crossed to my desk and opened my laptop. Willing my hands to stop shaking, I brought up my browser history and clicked on the last webpage I'd visited two days earlier when researching Vincent van Gogh for an art history paper. I chewed on a nail as I waited for the site to load.

When the first image came up, my heart skipped a beat. It was just as I'd thought and feared. The bold, dramatic brushstrokes and colours of van Gogh's *Poppy Field* were an exact match to the world I'd just been flung into.

How was it possible? What kind of force was inside me that made me open that shimmery doorway and *transport* myself like that? And the other question — the one that made me break into a cold sweat — was what should I do about it? If I told anyone, they would think I'd had some kind of psychotic meltdown. They wouldn't believe me, just like I hadn't believed Luke.

Luke.

At the thought of him, my stomach gave a queasy lurch. He was right.

I am *a witch.*

* * * *

On Monday morning, the last thing I wanted to do was go to school, but I needed to talk to Luke and I didn't know how else to contact him. That creep knew more about me than I knew myself, and I wanted answers. Luckily, history was first period, so I wouldn't have to wait long.

After the craziness I'd experienced in my room the day before, I'd lain flat on my back, staring up at the ceiling as I played it over and over again in my head. I tried to convince myself it was a hallucination. One second I'd been in my room, finally letting myself give in to the myriad emotions waging a war inside me, and the next, a window to another world had opened up, sucking me inside. And not just any world... A *painting.* There was just no way something like that could happen. No freakin' way.

But if it had been a hallucination, how did Luke know about it? And if he'd been telling the truth about what *I* could do...maybe his story about Mom sending his father into my mural was also true.

I shook my head. I should be questioning my own sanity for believing Luke.

Only I'd been inside van Gogh's *Poppy Field*, and it had been sickeningly real.

I hurried into the girls' washroom several minutes before the first bell rang, pulling my phone out as I went. For about the tenth time that morning, I dialled Aunt Karen's cell. If Mom had shared my curse or power or whatever it was, surely Aunt Karen knew something about it. But for the tenth time, it went to voice mail. *Damn.* Blowing out a breath, I left a message.

"Aunt Karen, *please* call me as soon as you get this." I hesitated, then took the plunge. "I didn't want to tell you this over voice mail but...something weird happened to me. Beyond weird. I need to talk to you. Call me back."

I ended the call. Well, that was that. I couldn't wait for my aunt to get out of her seminars and call me. I needed to know what the hell was going on, and right now Luke was my only source of information.

I splashed cold water on my face and patted it dry, then stared at my reflection in the mirror. My eyes were wide and panic-stricken. "What *am* I?" I whispered.

The door opened and shoes clicked on the chequered floor tiles. Trisha appeared at the sink beside me, smoothing down her cloud of bottle-blonde hair. She glared at me in the mirror, sparks shooting from her eyes.

"What's your problem?" I said.

"You are, bitch. I know what you're trying to do. You're trying to steal Luke from me."

The idea was so ridiculous that I had to laugh. "Oh, I am, am I? And what gave you that impression?"

She put her hands on her hips. Her snug fitting top rode up, baring her midriff and a glinting bellybutton ring. "Don't deny it. I heard how you got all cosy with him in the loft at Scott's party."

"Whatever you heard, it's wrong."

"I'm not going to let you have Luke. He's the hottest thing this school has seen in a long time." She looked me up and down. "He's not even your type. But you think you can do whatever you want, have whoever you want because you're a walking tragedy — nothing but a charity case. A cool guy like Luke won't want to be around you for long. He'll dump your sad little ass, just like Nick wanted to."

"That's a lie!" I said, my voice so loud it echoed off the bathroom walls. "And don't you dare talk about Nick."

She raised a perfectly manicured eyebrow. "My, my... The Ice Princess is getting mad. There's something you don't see every day."

I sunk my nails into my palms. Suddenly I found myself reacting to everything. And I knew it was all connected to this insane power I'd discovered.

"Look," I said through gritted teeth. "Nothing is going on between me and Luke."

Trisha dug into her bag. She withdrew a tube of lip gloss and began to apply it. She didn't speak again until she was finished. "Then why did you go to the loft with him?"

"I didn't. He followed me up there. I thought it was all part of your prank."

"Again with the prank crap? I told you already that I didn't pull any prank on you."

"Yeah, I know that now. And seriously, he's all yours. Just tell me... Do you know why he transferred? Did it have something to do with his father?"

She examined her French manicure. "I dunno. He might've said something about his dad moving away. I didn't really pay attention." Her head snapped up, suspicion carved into her sharp features. "Why do you even care?"

"Research for his yearbook profile."

"Oh, come on. You don't expect me to believe that."

The bathroom door swung open and in stepped Roxy. She stopped, looking from me to Trisha and back again. "Jules? What's going on?"

Trisha scowled. "Your bestie is lying through her teeth. That's what's going on. She's trying to tell me she's not stealing Luke Mercer from me."

Roxy let out a laugh that was half-annoyed, half-amused. "Oh, please. Anybody with half a brain knows she's not." As her laughter trailed off, she narrowed her eyes at Trisha. "If anyone's in the habit of trying to steal guys, it's you."

"I don't know *what* you're talking about. I—"

But Roxy wasn't finished. "Now get out," she said in a steely voice. "I want to talk to Jules alone."

"Whatever. I've got better things to do than stay in here with you two losers."

With one last glare in my direction, Trisha stalked out of the room. As soon as the door closed behind her, Roxy pounced on me. "Hey, what's the deal? You didn't call me back yesterday. I tried your cell a bunch of times."

"Sorry," I said. "I wasn't feeling well." *That* was the understatement of the year.

"We need to talk about what happened Saturday. I know you said it was no big deal, but you seemed really freaked out."

I shrugged. "It's fine. I'm fine."

Roxy let out a sigh. "Listen... I can't always tell what's going on in that head of yours, but I know something's wrong now. Are you still upset about your locket? Did anyone find it?"

"No, I checked with the office a few minutes ago. Nothing." Before I could say anything else, my cell phone vibrated in my pocket, signalling a new text message. Hope bloomed in my chest. Maybe Aunt Karen was finally getting back to me.

When I looked at the screen, though, I saw a number I didn't recognise. And it didn't take a genius to figure out who'd sent the message.

We're not done talking, witch. Meet me in the quad. Five minutes.

I tossed the phone in my bag, the hope turning into renewed determination mixed with a pinch of annoyance. I was more than ready to find out what Luke knew. I just hated the fact that a total ass was the only one who could shed some light on what was happening to me.

"You know," I said to Roxy, "I think I'm going to go home for the day. Still not feeling so hot." *And I don't know how to tell you I'm a freak who can make paintings come to life.*

"Jules, wait."

"I gotta go. I'll talk to you tomorrow." I felt a twinge of guilt as I rushed out of the bathroom. I knew it wasn't fair to keep my best friend in the dark, but I couldn't tell her what was going on — at least, not yet. Not until I understood it myself.

I slipped out of the side door of the school just as the bell rang and hurried across the quad. Students who had a free period loitered on benches or sprawled on the huge expanse of lawn. I'd just reached the centre of the quad when I heard footsteps behind me. A moment later, a hand clasped my shoulder.

I whirled around and found myself face-to-face with Luke. As usual, he was dressed in head-to-toe black. His dark hair stood up in wild tufts.

He flashed me a chilling smile. "I see you got my text. Wasn't sure if you'd skip class, though."

"Well, I want to talk to you, too." I paused. "How did you get my cell number anyway?"

"Some chick from our history class. Told her you borrowed my textbook and I wanted to remind you to bring it to class. So, you finally ready to get my old man back?"

"I don't know anything about your father," I said, struggling to keep my voice from rising again. "I'm here because I want some answers."

His eyebrows winged up. "Answers?"

"Yeah," I said, "since you seem to know so much about me and my mother."

He laughed, a hollow sound. "I know people call you the Ice Princess."

I balled my hands into fists. God, I was tired of hearing that. "That's just a stupid name Trisha made up. And you know what I'm talking about. I need you to tell me everything about this...ability I have."

"And why would you need me to explain your own freaky power to you?"

"Because," I said through clenched teeth, "I don't know anything about it."

"Of course you do. My father saw it with his own eyes."

"And I *told* you that I don't remember!" I was rapidly losing patience with him. If he didn't give me some answers soon, I was afraid I'd explode.

He looked at me for a long moment, his hands jammed in his pockets. Finally, he said, "You really expect me to believe you didn't know you're a witch?"

"Yes. It's only the last couple of days I've noticed that I can do weird things. Yesterday I..." I licked my dry lips and tried again. "I think I accidentally performed magic." The words sounded ridiculous when I said them out loud, but I didn't know how else to describe what I'd done.

"Really? What exactly did you do?"

I hesitated again. How could I explain opening a doorway to a van Gogh painting?

"Come on...out with it."

Speaking in a rush now, I recounted the bizarre events in my room as best I could. He listened with a neutral expression on his face, but when I was done, he threw his head back and let out a scornful laugh. "All this from the girl who said she doesn't know anything about witchcraft."

"I *don't* know anything about it!" I said, my face burning. "I told you... It was an accident. It was like I had this emotional breakdown and...and it just *happened.* I've never lost control like that before." And I never wanted to experience it again.

"Right," Luke said dryly. "Because you're the Ice Princess. And what about your mother? She never filled you in on your family's dark little secret?"

"No."

"Well, she knew about it, all right." He rubbed his jaw, a cocky smile lifting the corners of his mouth.

I tried to ignore the pain that stabbed my heart. I couldn't think about that until I knew the whole story. "Just tell me everything."

"Fine," he said. "But after I do that, you're going to bring back my father."

"I promise that if my mother really did send him somewhere, I'll do everything I can to get him back."

"Oh, there's no *if* about it, Princess."

"What do you mean? Did you see it happen?" I stared at him, my heart hammering in my chest.

"She told me about it herself."

"She told you? When?"

He let out a low whistle. "You have no idea what went down during that fire, do you? Never even guessed what really happened to your boyfriend."

I had to take several deep breaths before I could speak again. "And how would you know anything about that day?"

He took a few steps forward, closing the gap between us. His blue eyes were steady on mine. "Because I was there."

Chapter Four

"What do you mean, you were there?" I asked. He was lying. He had to be. There was no way he'd been at my house on the day of the fire. I would've known about it somehow…wouldn't I?

"Just what I said. I was there…inside your house."

A couple of jocks ran down the path towards us, cracking jokes. Luke grabbed my arm and steered me to a bench on a grassy knoll. He sat and gestured for me to do the same.

"I don't understand. *Why* were you there?" I crossed my arms over my chest, refusing to sit.

"My dad was missing, and I was pretty sure your mother knew something about it."

My head was spinning. "What? Why in the world would you think that? And what do you know about the fire? What happened to Nick?"

He held up a hand. "Calm down, Princess. One thing at a time. Man, I still can't believe I have to fill you in on your own family's twisted magic."

"Well, believe it," I said, straining for patience. "I can't help your father if you don't. Tell me exactly what happened."

"Then I'll start at the beginning, so you'll understand. The very beginning. Sit down."

I sat on the other end of the bench so that there was a wide gap between us. With my back and shoulders tense, I turned to him. "All right. I'm listening."

"You remember what I told you about my old man, Tom, seeing you flip out at me?"

I nodded.

"Well, he told me it was the craziest thing he'd ever seen in his life. You were standing there screaming at me, your face all red, then you closed your eyes. The next thing he knew, this glowing *thing* just appeared out of nowhere."

"What kind of thing?" My voice sounded faraway, as if I were wearing earplugs.

"He said it was kind of in the shape of a door, but it wasn't solid. It just floated there or some shit. And he could see right into it."

"What did he see?"

Luke lifted a shoulder in a shrug. "I don't think he knew what he was looking at. It was just this blur. So friggin' bright it gave him a headache."

A sensation like ice-cold fingers moved up and down my spine. I had no idea what kind of insane world I'd unlocked when I had been five, but Luke's description sounded an awful lot like the rectangular opening that had appeared in my bedroom.

"Then," Luke continued, "some kind of freaky wind started pulling on me. My father said it was like it was trying to pull me into the glowy thing. My teddy bear got sucked right into the hole."

Oh my God. That explained the flashes I'd been getting of the stuffed animal sailing through the air. It had really happened. Had I blocked out everything from that day except for that single moment? "So, what stopped you from getting sucked in, too?" I croaked, my throat as dry as sawdust.

"By then, Tom was shaking you, yelling for you to stop it. And just like that" — he snapped his fingers — "the hole disappeared."

I leapt up from the bench, unable to sit still any longer. A sick feeling twisted my stomach. "Then what happened?"

"Well, your mom must've seen the whole thing from the door or window or whatever because she came over and told Tom to get his hands off you. And *you* said you just wanted me to leave you alone, that you'd wished for me to go away."

He leaned back, his eyes still trained on me. "None of that rings a bell?"

"No," I managed.

"After that, Tom couldn't wait to get us out of that neighbourhood and away from you. Look... I don't remember much from that time, either. Jesus, we were only five." He shook his head. "But my father made sure I knew what happened that day. He told the story over and over, and I swear, it got more and more dramatic each time. He's convinced you scarred me for life and that you caused all my 'behavioural problems', as he calls them." He laughed humourlessly. "Okay, so I've been in a shit load of trouble over the years, but the truth is that I think the old man is more messed up than I am. Anyway, at the beginning of the summer, just before I got nailed for that holdup, your mom was on the news a lot."

"Right. She was promoting the play she'd directed." Despite the warm September sun beating down on me, chills raced over my skin. I pressed my back against the tree next to the bench and rubbed my bare arms.

"Yeah. So, Tom started to get really obsessed with her, saying things like, *'There's that witch's mother on TV again. Goddamn girl is all to blame for the way you ended up, Lucas.'* Then he would mutter these crazy threats like *'One of these days I'm gonna make her pay for ruining our lives.'* I just ignored him. Like I said, I'd heard the story so many times, but I'd never believed it. I just thought he was messed up in the head." He laughed again. "The old man's a bit of an alcoholic, you know? I thought it was the booze talking again. Anyway, I came home late one night, went straight to bed and in the morning realized he hadn't come home. I figured he'd finally lost it and went after you."

I put a hand to my stomach, feeling nauseated. I opened my mouth to deny all of it, to defend myself or to tell him he was making it all up, but no sound came out. I couldn't form the words because I didn't know if I believed them. I had made a painting come to life just the day before. As much as I wanted to believe that it was a hallucination or a dream…it'd been all too real.

Questions tumbled through my mind. *Isn't it possible that if I could transport myself into a painting, that I might have tried to do the same thing to Luke all those years ago and blocked out the memory? But then why would Mom keep it from me? And if Tom Mercer confronted her, why didn't she warn me that he was out for revenge?* Unless… Unless she hadn't had time.

"So you came to my house looking for him?" I asked.

"Exactly. And what did I find when I got to your place? No sign of my father. Just your boy Nick and

Charlotte the Great, who insisted that Tom hadn't been by. She was cool as a cucumber, but I knew she was hiding something. So I told her I wasn't leaving until I got some answers." His words came out in a rush and his face flushed with anger. "Well, that really got Nick all riled up. He shoved me, so I shoved back. I had to defend myself, right? But *then* he took a swing at me." Luke leaned forward and spat on the ground.

I scrubbed my face with my hands. It'd always amazed me how quickly Nick—usually so warm and easy-going—could succumb to his temper when provoked.

"I dodged it easily and punched him. Now Mommy Dearest didn't seem to like Loverboy getting hurt, so she cried out that she'd sent Tom into your mural and—"

"Wait!" I held up a hand. "She actually told you that? What else did she say?"

A scowl darkened his face. "She said my old man had come to see her, drunk as a skunk, and when he'd threatened her, she'd accidentally sent him into the mural. Like I said, your ability is a family affair."

My hands trembled. I pressed them together to keep them still. If it were true, my whole life was a lie. My mother and I were freaks of nature. And she'd kept it from me.

"And the fire?" I closed my eyes, dreading the answer. "How did it start?"

"Grease fire in the kitchen. Your mother should've been more careful with her cooking oil."

"B-but… B-but we were going out to an awards dinner," I stuttered. "She wouldn't have been cooking anything."

"Well, she was," he insisted, his eyes hard.

"So then what happened?" I asked bitterly. "You got out in time while Mom and Nick burned to death?"

"Your boy breathed in smoke. He was unconscious. I got down low, so I didn't breathe in as much as he did. I crawled to the back door to get out."

"And you didn't try to help him?" I pushed off the tree, itching to take hold of his neck and squeeze as hard as I could.

"I didn't have to," he sneered. "Your mom took care of that. She was already at his side, going on about how she had to get him out of there. Then she closed her eyes and moaned something about 'Jules' mural'. And that's when another one of those glowing doors showed up. She was freakin' obsessed with that mural."

I dropped my hands limply to my sides. My stomach went all topsy-turvy like it did when I was on a roller coaster. "Are you saying...?" I trailed off, scared to even utter the words.

"I'm saying he was sucked up into the mural. I'm just glad I didn't get trapped in there, too."

I took a deep, ragged breath. "And my mother?" The fire investigators had found human remains, but they'd had difficulty identifying them. Another point I wished I'd questioned.

He scratched the back of his neck, looking uncomfortable for the first time. "I don't know if it was your mother's magic or what, but as soon as that portal opened, the fire got out of control, like crazy out of control. Never seen anything like it. Suddenly everything was crashing down around us."

"And?"

"A beam fell on top of your mom, and the door to mural land closed. By that time, there was no way I could reach her. I barely made it out myself. Luckily, I was close enough to the back door that I could escape in time. Talk about a close call, though. Another second and I would've died in there, too."

I couldn't feel my legs. When my knees buckled, I grabbed the edge of the bench to keep from collapsing. A part of me wanted to focus on the anger that hummed in my veins at the image of Luke running away while my mother burned to death. But another part surged with hope.

"Are you sure Nick got out in time?"

"Yeah," he said impatiently. "I saw him get pulled into that crazy door."

"Did you go look at the mural? Like, did you *see* either one of them in there?" Panicked thoughts raced through my head. "If your dad and Nick are trapped in there, wouldn't we somehow see them in the painting?"

He frowned. "No, I didn't *see* them. But that doesn't mean they're not in there. Jesus, I don't know how this works."

"Well, I don't either," I protested.

"But you can figure it out." He rose from the bench. "I need you to go down to that mural with me, get my dad out and maybe Loverboy at the same time. Everybody's happy."

"No," I repeated, "everybody is *not* happy. For the past two months, I've been thinking Nick was dead, when really he's been trapped in some fantasy land! You couldn't have gotten in touch right after this happened?"

"Right after it happened," he said in a cold voice, "I was picked up for juvie. You don't get a whole lot of telephone privileges in there. And it's not exactly something you write a letter about."

I frowned, not buying it. Why hadn't he tried harder to contact me, not knowing if his dad was hurt...or worse? Something didn't add up. "And... And you couldn't have led with the fact that you saw Nick getting out of the fire?"

"My first priority was my father, not your boyfriend."

I rubbed my eyes. "I can't believe this. This is insane. You shouldn't have been in my house in the first place." I stepped forward again and started pounding on his chest. "I lost everything because of you!"

He stopped me with little effort. "Get a hold of yourself. The fire was an accident, and if I'm not mistaken, this whole thing started because of *you*. But now you have a chance to save Nick *and* my dad." He paused. "And if you get my old man back, I'll tell you something else your mom said that day."

"What are you talking about?"

"A secret she'd just found out about the origins of your magic. She thought she was close to finding a way to get rid of it...forever."

My body went completely still. Why would she trust Luke with that? Was he lying? "What secret?"

"Nope. Not yet. Not until my dad is out of that painting. Now, do we have a deal?"

I forced deep breaths through my lungs. I needed to stay in control, even though I wanted to shake Luke until he told me what Mom had discovered. "Fine. But even if you're right about them being in the mural, I don't know exactly how to get in there."

"Then we'll play it by ear. We'll go to the mural and maybe it will come to you." He flashed me a twisted grin. "Time for you to bring out your witchy powers, Parsons."

* * * *

I must be crazy, I thought as Luke's car sped through the streets of St. Peter's. I sneaked a glance at his profile. His jaw was clenched, his knuckles white on the steering wheel. This whole thing was crazy. How could people just go into a painting? And what happened to them once they'd been in there for a long time? I'd only been in the poppy field for a few seconds. If Luke was telling the truth, Tom and Nick had been in my snowy village for two months.

Luke stopped the car in front of the mural. "Here we are."

My legs still felt like Jell-O, but I forced myself to stand and face the long wall that boasted my artwork. The wall, which was topped with a metal railing, bordered the sloping hill that led to the community of Joseph Heights. I ran my eyes over the painting, taking it all in — the red and brown cottages spread out over a deep blanket of pure white snow, the icy river winding through silvery-green fir trees and my favourite part, the grand mountains that rose in the background, their white-speckled peaks glistening against a pink-and-yellow-tinged sky.

I squinted at the group of villagers interspersed throughout the painting, draped in winter cloaks. There were no extra people, from what I could see. *Is Nick really in there?* I bit my lip, recalling how I'd opened some sort of portal to the van Gogh painting. So as ludicrous as Luke's story was, it seemed within the realm of possibility that I could also create an opening to my village.

"How quaint," Luke said, sarcasm lacing his words.

"Shut up," I muttered, staring at the wall. "Let me think."

My heart thundered in my chest. So what was I supposed to do? The crazy trip yesterday had been a total accident. I didn't understand how I'd made the painting come alive. All I knew was that I'd been overcome with the need to be somewhere else, then the bubble had appeared, pulling me inside. Could I get into a work of art just by wishing it? And even if I could find the way in, there was no guarantee Nick and Tom had survived after being in there for so long. I shuddered at the thought of what a real-life version of my painting would actually be like.

Luke shuffled back and forth in front of me, grunting. "Come on. We're burning daylight here."

"I *told* you that I don't know how to do this." I frowned at him. "Why are you in such a hurry to get your dad back, anyway? Sounds like there's no love lost between you two, the way you were talking."

Something flashed in his eyes. "Never mind that. Just do your thing. You said you had a meltdown yesterday, right? Maybe you need to have another one. Get mad or sad or something."

"Right." I took a deep breath. Emotions did seem to be key in all this. And giving in to them should be easy enough, considering my mood of late.

"Want some help with that?" Luke quirked an eyebrow. "I'm pretty good at pissing people off, you know."

"Oh, I know," I said. "But I think I can manage it on my own."

"I really don't mind. Hmm... How about... Oh, I've got it. Why don't you think about how you felt when your house burned down? That must've been really hard for you, thinking your mom and boyfriend bit the dust in there. But— Oh, yeah." He whistled. "The thing is that everyone is saying you were so calm about the whole thing."

"No, not that. I don't want to think about that."

"Why not?" He grabbed my chin, forcing me to look at him. "It's the perfect thing to get you riled up. You can't tell me it didn't hurt like hell. You must've worked hard to keep all your feelings inside. But we're old friends, Jules. You can tell me how you *really* felt. I heard you got there in time to see the roof collapse. Didn't that make you want to scream and bawl your eyes out?"

I swatted his hand away and took a step back. "No." My voice was a choked whisper. "It didn't."

Wrapped in that protective coating, which had seemed to numb me from the inside out, I hadn't screamed or cried. But I wanted to now. I wanted to scream at Luke for bringing up the fire. And, at the same time, I felt the overpowering urge to cry.

"Why not?" he sneered. "What are you, a robot? Or you just didn't give a damn about Mommy and your Loverboy?"

"Shut up!" I pushed on his chest so hard that he stumbled back. "I loved them. I loved them so much I can barely stand to think about them. So don't you dare tell me I didn't care!"

Tears filled my eyes. I let myself be lost in them, let the grief and anger at long last consume me. My body shook with sobs that had me gasping for air. The tears rolled down my cheeks one after another, and with them came the deep-seated need to be with Nick again.

My vision blurred. Once again, an unseen energy forced my eyes closed. I heard the sound of crunching snow, and a blast of cold air hit my body.

Then a shrill ringing eclipsed everything else. The sensation of spinning fell away. The sounds of winter disappeared.

When I could open my eyes, I stared at the mural for a few seconds, dazed, before I realized it was my cell phone that had gone off. And it was still ringing. I fumbled it out of my pocket. The number had a New York area code.

"Aunt Karen?"

"Julia!" she said, sounding breathless. "Are you all right? I got your message. My phone wasn't charged and I was in back-to-back seminars. What happened?"

I glanced at Luke, who was standing a few feet away, an enraged expression on his face. I turned my back on him and said, "I, uh, don't really know how to explain it. And I know this is going to sound weird, but do you know anything about…magic?"

A beat of silence before my aunt spoke again. When she did, her voice was edged with fear. "Did something happen to your locket?"

I swallowed. "I lost it. How did you know?"

Instead of answering, she said, "Julia, you have to get that locket back. You have no idea how powerful it is."

"Powerful? What are you talking about?"

"Have you been getting upset at all? Sad? Angry?"

"Ah, yeah. All of the above." My stomach churned.

"And did anything else happen?"

"Yes. Apparently, I can do this insane thing with pictures."

"You— You opened one?" Her voice was frantic now. "Did you send anyone in there?"

"Just myself," I said bitterly.

"Thank God you were able to get yourself out of there. You—"

"Aunt Karen, what the hell is happening to me? What do you know?"

"Julia, listen to me very carefully. That locket was suppressing your ability and, without it, you're a danger to yourself and other people. Now I want you to go home and wait for me there. I'm taking the next flight out, so I'll be back in a few hours."

My breathing was shallow, and I felt like I was going to throw up again. But I couldn't dwell on the fact that my aunt had known about my ability all along—*and* that my necklace had been imbued with some kind of magic. I needed to tell her about Nick.

"Wait! Aunt Karen, I think Nick is alive."

There was a sharp intake of breath. "Why do you think that?"

"There's this guy, Luke Mercer—"

"Wait a second. *Luke Mercer* found you?"

"You know him?"

"I remember him from a long time ago," she said, her voice tight. "Well, at least what your mother told me. What did he say to you?"

She'd known about Luke, too, and she'd said nothing? Why would she keep me in the dark for so long? I gritted my teeth, biting back the urge to scream. Instead, I gave her the basic outline of Luke's story. "We're down at the mural now. If Nick and Luke's dad are in there, I have to get them back."

"Absolutely not. It's too dangerous. There are things you need to know before traipsing in after them. You have no idea how to control your power, and you can't just go in there without being prepared. You'll put them both in danger. There are consequences, Julia!"

"Well, then tell me what they are!"

"I can't and won't do it over the phone. Promise me you'll stay put until I get home."

I was itching to find Nick. I'd already felt the pull of the mural just before the phone rang. But my aunt was right. I was totally clueless about my newfound power, and the last thing I wanted to do was put Nick at risk. So I sighed. "Fine. I'll wait for you."

I ended the call and turned back to Luke. "I need you to take me home."

"What? No way. That wasn't the deal! Your painting there started to do this weird shimmering thing, but it stopped when your friggin' phone rang. Now get back over there and try again."

"Hey, I want to do this as much as you do. Believe me. But my aunt says it's not safe to go in there until I know everything. And since *she* seems to know all about it," I added, bitterness returning to my voice, "I'm going to go wait for her."

His eyes flashed with annoyance. "Oh, so *now* someone in your family decides to fill you in. Give me a break."

"Shut up," I said again. "Just think about it. What if I get in there and can't get your dad out? You can wait a little bit longer, and once I know exactly what I'm dealing with, I'll try again. I'll call you when I'm ready."

He started towards me, his hands clenched into fists. I thought he was going to argue again, but then he stopped and let out a grunt. "Fine. We'll do it your way. I'll give you until tomorrow morning. If I don't hear from you by then, I'm coming to find you."

"I'll call," I repeated firmly.

Luke stepped over to his car, muttering under his breath. I glanced back at the mural before following, my heart heavy with the knowledge that Nick could be so close, yet so far away.

Chapter Five

After Luke dropped me off, I washed my face in the upstairs bathroom. With water droplets clinging to my chin, I stared at myself in the mirror, at the face so like Mom's, with its olive tone and oval shape, and at the hair so like hers, with its silvery blonde strands cutting swathes through the dark brown.

What was I? What had *she* been?

My mind reeled as I weaved into my bedroom and collapsed on the bed. I'd almost gone into my mural — and Aunt Karen knew what I could do. She'd known all along. My whole life was a lie. A mix of anguish and disbelief hung over me like the dark ribbons of fog that curled off the coast.

I wanted to talk to Nick. I needed to hear his voice reassuring me, feel his comforting arms around me. And if I could find him... If I could get him back, I'd make that dream a reality.

Weighed down by an emotional and physical exhaustion that seeped into every bone, I sank under the covers. After a while, I drifted into a broken sleep that was plagued with disturbing visions of Mom and Nick, their flesh melting into pools as the fire ravaged them with amorphous hands.

I woke, gasping for air. When my heart rate finally slowed, I checked my cell. Aunt Karen had texted me her flight info. She was due to arrive soon.

I got up to monitor the driveway from my window seat. The sun was a golden disc that burned through wispy clouds streaked with blue. While I watched some kids run down the street, their giddy shouts carried on the wind, I thought of my mother. Why hadn't she told me how freakishly dangerous I was? How could she have ever trusted me around other people, knowing I had this ability?

When the Corolla pulled in the driveway, I flew down the stairs and flung open the door just as my aunt reached the front stoop. She lifted her head, her forehead creased with concern. "Julia, what—?"

I didn't give her a chance to finish. "Am I some kind of witch?" I blurted.

Her mouth opened and closed a couple of times. Then she shook her head. "Not here. Inside."

I moved aside so she could enter the house. As soon as she put her bag down, she grabbed my hand and pulled me into the living room. "Let's sit down."

I perched on the edge of the sofa. She sat beside me, keeping my hand in hers. It was cool to the touch, despite the warm afternoon.

"Just tell me," I pleaded. "What was Mom? What am I?"

"Julia, did you...?" My aunt took a deep breath. Fear was written all over her face. "Did you try to go into the mural after I talked to you?"

"No. I—I think I could've gone in, but I waited for you."

"Good. That's good. The thing is, honey, none of this was supposed to happen."

"Stop avoiding the question." I snatched my hand away. "Just tell me what I am! For God's sake, Aunt Karen, I was *inside* a van Gogh painting!"

Her eyes widened, no doubt stunned because I'd never yelled at her before. When she spoke, her own voice was soft and shaky in comparison. "Yes, you're a kind of witch. A Vista witch."

"A *what*?"

"A Vista," she repeated. "You have the power to open doorways into pictures or paintings. And once a doorway is open, it takes whoever is near and pulls them right in. You don't need to be in close proximity to the actual picture to open it, but the closer you are, the easier it is to access. You just have to know it exists and you can create a door."

"Like a portal?"

"You can think of it like that. Usually Vistas will conjure an opening to whatever picture they last saw — or one that's been on their mind. It can be anything that was created by an artist's hand."

Which explained why I'd created a portal to van Gogh's painting, having been looking at it on the Internet a couple of days before, and why Mom had opened a door to my mural. She and I had talked about it the day before the fire.

A dull, throbbing sensation wound around my head, squeezing it like an elastic band. "This can't be happening."

"You come from a long line of Vistas, Julia. Your mom was one and so was your maternal grandfather."

I sat stock-still, staring at her with my mouth hanging open. "Oh my God," I said when I was finally able to speak again, "this thing runs in our family?"

"Yes. Your grandfather's fear during the mine explosion made him open up a portal and a couple of the miners went through."

"So those stories were true?"

She nodded. "Everyday stresses and frustrations aren't normally strong enough to bring on a Vista's power. It has to be triggered by extreme emotions."

"Yeah, I found that out the hard way," I muttered.

She gave me a sympathetic smile before continuing. "When you were born, your mother didn't know for sure if you were a Vista. Sometimes the ability to create doors doesn't show up until the person is older, and sometimes it skips a generation. But it's only ever a firstborn who inherits the magic."

"So that's why you didn't become one."

"Right. Anyway, she knew for sure you were one when you got so mad at the Mercer boy that you opened a painting."

The blood drained from my face. "So it really happened? Luke was telling the truth?"

She nodded, looking deathly pale herself. "You'd just found out about your dad's accident. You were upset and confused, and Luke? Well, he was in the wrong place at the wrong time."

"At first I thought it was some sick joke, but then I went into that poppy field and…" My voice grew thick. "And I feel like I'm losing it."

"That's because you're not wearing the locket anymore."

My hand flew to the hollow of my throat, my breath hitching. "What did the locket do?"

Aunt Karen glanced down at her hands, twisted together in her lap. When she lifted her head again, her eyes were dark with worry. "It was charmed to suppress strong emotions in whoever wears it. Your mom used to wear it, to control her own magic, but after the incident with Luke, she thought it was better for you to have its protection instead. The spell on the locket was designed so that the wearer is drawn to it and never wants to take it off. So…it was a struggle for your mom to give it up, but she knew it was the right thing to do."

I sprang from the sofa and looked at my aunt in horror. "She…the…" I sputtered, unable to form a coherent thought. "I've been controlled by a piece of jewellery almost my whole life? Everything I've thought and felt — or didn't feel — has been a lie?"

"No, of course not —"

"It feels like it!"

"The locket only restrained your most extreme emotions. You were still able to feel things."

"Just not the most important things, right? That's why I couldn't cry after the fire." The thought of having my free will taken away caused a wave of bitterness to roll over me. "How could Mom do that to me?"

"Please, Julia, you can't get upset."

But heat flooded my face and my throat burned with the sharp taste of resentment. "Well, excuse me if I don't know how to keep from getting upset. Apparently, I was never given the chance to learn that skill on my own!"

Aunt Karen crossed to me and put her hands on my shoulders. She held my gaze, her eyes pleading with me. "You have to use the techniques your mother used to control her feelings — deep breaths, counting to ten and things like that. I know she mentioned them to you. Please," she repeated. "You know by now how dangerous your emotions are."

I knew she was right. I had no desire to open a portal again, at least, not until I was ready to go after Nick. I inhaled and exhaled several times, and eventually my anger began to dissipate like the slow leak of air from a balloon. When I'd gained some semblance of composure, Aunt Karen walked to the kitchen and gestured for me to follow.

"Sit down," she said. "I'll make you some herbal tea. It'll help settle your nerves."

I opened my mouth to argue that all the tea in China couldn't help me now, but she was still talking as she put the kettle on.

"You have to understand, honey. Your mom gave you the necklace for protection, so you wouldn't hurt yourself or other people. She didn't make the decision lightly. She did it because it was necessary. And it worked, just like it'd worked for her. It kept your strongest emotions at bay and your magic was never triggered again."

"Until I lost the locket."

"Yes. When the locket came off, the protection was gone. Without it, you were able to feel the full extent of your grief."

Yeah, I'd felt it all right. It'd struck me like a sucker punch in the gut. "And what about my memory of the thing with Luke when I was a kid? Did it take that away, too?"

"I think it's possible. Memories are tied to emotions, so the locket may have repressed that, too." She shot me a glance as she set mugs on the counter. "If that's the case, don't be surprised if the memory of that day starts to come back to you."

"Actually, I think part of it already has." I told her about seeing the bear fly through the air, and how the image matched what Luke had told me. "He also said Mom was close to finding a way to get rid of the Vista magic forever. Is that true? Is there something more permanent than the locket?"

Aunt Karen shook her head. "Not that I know of. She didn't mention anything to me."

I massaged my forehead. "Maybe he was lying about it then."

"And what else did he say?" she asked. "What does he know about the fire?"

"He said it was a grease fire in the kitchen. But that doesn't make sense. Mom wouldn't have been cooking."

"Julia…" Aunt Karen shut the cupboard door very slowly and turned around. "I don't know if that's true or not. But I think I might know how the fire got out of control so fast."

"How?"

"Well, the force of opening a portal can cause a shift in the elements surrounding it, making them worse. For instance, if a Vista conjured a door in a place where a light rain is falling, the rain will become a torrential downpour. Or if there are flames, the fire will spread much more quickly than it would otherwise. It would've been so powerful that not even the opening to your winter mural could cool it. And the longer the fire went on, the more intense the heat." She paused. "That could explain why the human remains were destroyed beyond recognition."

I swallowed. I didn't want to think about what had happened to Mom's body as the fire wore on. "So, what you're saying is that by using her magic, Mom made the fire *worse*? Why didn't she just drag Nick out when she could? Why did she have to send him into the mural at all?"

Aunt Karen sighed. "Because she was being led by her emotions. If she was terrified, her automatic response would be to create the door. That's how the magic works. Isn't that what you experienced with the poppy field?"

"Yeah, I guess. I started crying and couldn't stop...and that bubble was just *there*." I pushed at my hair, struggling to get my breathing under control again. "How can you even call it magic? It's more like a curse."

"Your mother agreed with you," my aunt said with a grim smile as she brought the mugs over to the table.

"It's not right." My voice was a fierce whisper now. "She should've had something to protect her, too. Why didn't she charm another necklace or something after she gave me hers?"

"Oh, she didn't charm the necklace. Vistas aren't that kind of witch. They only have the power to open worlds, not write spells or anything like that. But years before, your mom had tracked down a witch who could charm objects. The problem was that your mom couldn't find the witch when she needed her again. So she did the best she could. She had to work on containing her emotions. She had actually become pretty good at it."

My heart beat a mile a minute as I tried to process this new information. Charmed objects, witches... I wrapped my hands around the mug to stop them from shaking. "When exactly did she have the locket charmed?"

"She was about your age. When we were growing up, our parents told us all these stories about the Vistas in our family who'd opened portals. And because they knew Charlotte had the potential for the same kind of magic, they constantly warned her about letting her emotions get out of control." My aunt stared out of the window at the afternoon sun, her eyes taking on a faraway look. "But they not only warned her, they also tried to protect her."

"How?"

"By keeping a close watch on her, giving her a strict curfew, forbidding her to do certain activities or hang around with anyone they thought could be a bad influence. But it backfired. Charlotte started to resent them, said they were stifling her. Things were strained between them. Then one night, things came to a head." Aunt Karen grimaced. "When Charlotte was your age, she snuck out to a college party and didn't come home until three in the morning."

I raised my eyebrows. Mom sneaking out to a party? It sounded so unlike her. "I'm guessing that was way past curfew."

"It was. Mom and Dad grounded her for a month and all the anger and resentment Charlotte had been holding in just burst out of her."

"Oh my God," I whispered. "She opened a picture?"

"A movie poster. It was for some awful B movie called *Dark Stones*. Mom and Dad were sucked right into it."

I let out a sound that was a cross between a gasp and a laugh. It was bizarre to imagine Mom as a rebellious teen who'd transported her own parents.

"It's true. Good thing for Dad that he knew how to get back out."

"This is unbelievable." I shook my head, dazed.

"And after that, Charlotte was so freaked out by what she'd done that she was willing to do anything to make her power go away. So she found the witch and asked her to create a spell."

"But why didn't she tell me any of this?"

"She didn't want to handle you with kid gloves, like our parents did with her. By harping on the dangers of emotions like they did, they'd made things worse. Besides, the locket was containing your magic, and she just thought you'd be better off not knowing—and not remembering what happened with Luke."

"And she didn't see a problem with me wanting to become an artist?" I snorted. "Seems to be the worst possible profession for someone who can open pictures."

"Not as long as you had the necklace. And she made sure you did. You were drawn to wearing it, as per the spell, so she knew you'd be safe." Aunt Karen reached over and squeezed my arm. "I think subconsciously you were using art as a way to express the emotions that the locket was filtering."

I frowned. "But at the same time creating something that could be used as a portal. Kind of a catch-22, isn't it?"

"Julia—"

"I can't believe you guys kept me in the dark all my life." My heart beat a loud, staccato rhythm in my chest. "And that I had to find out what I am from some juvenile delinquent who's practically threatening to hurt me if I don't rescue his father—who, by the way, has it in for me!"

"Julia, look at me."

I did as she asked. Her green eyes were earnest. "Your mother did the best she could. After you had the locket, you became such a calm, easy-going child. Your magic was under control, and you were able to enjoy life without being burdened by it, not having to think about it all the time like she did when she was growing up. She wanted things to be different for you. And as for Tom Mercer? He seemed to be a thing of the past too. It didn't occur to her that he would come threatening her years later."

I pushed at my tangled hair with a frustrated sigh. "Well, Luke is determined to make my life a living hell until I get his father back. But I can deal with him. I just want Nick back." I took a deep breath. "Do you think Mom really sent him into the mural?"

"It's possible." She gave me a small, rueful smile. "We're talking about the girl who sent her own parents into a *Dark Stones* poster. And if she was trying to save Nick, it could've happened."

I shook my head. "It's so weird to think of Mom losing her cool."

Aunt Karen's smile widened just a little. "She had lots of practice controlling herself. To me, it sounds like her magic was triggered when Tom Mercer paid her a visit."

"Why didn't she bring him back out of the mural after she sent him in?"

"I don't know. Maybe she didn't have a chance."

"There's no sign of either of them being in there, though. Like, I can't see them in the painting."

"No," Aunt Karen said. "And you wouldn't. That's not how it works. If someone goes through a door into the world of a painting, they don't just appear in it, because the artist didn't create them. So everything will still look the same from the outside. But there's something more important you need to know." Her sombre eyes met mine. "Once the mural is painted over, your magic won't be strong enough to open a door out of it. The painting will go dark. Nobody inside will be able to survive."

My frustration melted away, replaced by a fear so cold it chilled me to the bone. "Then I'll do anything to get them back before that happens. What are these other consequences you were talking about?"

"As a Vista, you're immune to the magic inside the world of a picture. But if Nick and Tom are trapped in the painting...they won't be themselves." Aunt Karen watched me intently. "They might believe they actually belong in there. And if they do, you can't open up a portal and send them back to the real world until they remember who they are."

"What? Why?"

She bit her lip. "They won't survive the journey home. That's what happened when your Great-Grandmother Edna accidentally transported herself and her younger brother Cecil into a painting. When she tried to send him back out through a portal before he remembered who he was, he died. It was as if Cecil had become part of the painting and trying to take him out of it killed him."

My voice came out hoarse and ragged. "You can't be serious. That's totally screwed up." I swallowed. "Okay, so when Nick sees me, he'll remember. Or I'll remind him who he is."

She gave a solemn nod. "You can, but a memory trigger will probably work better."

"A memory trigger?" I echoed.

"Like a personal item, something that reminds the person of home, a memento of some kind…anything to keep them grounded and keep their memories intact. Dad discovered the power of personal objects as memory triggers when he and Mom got sucked into *Dark Stones*. Mom forgot who she was, so he tried to get her to remember by giving her back her wedding ring. He had it in his pocket, had taken it to get cleaned. Not long after, she was herself again."

"If Nick had his wallet with him, would that help him?"

"It would. And I hope that he did. But just in case, you should bring a memory trigger for Nick. And Luke will need to get one for Tom, too. Each person needs their own trigger because it has to be personal to them, and they each need to hold on to the item for it to work."

"And these items will help them remember who they are?"

"They should. But I don't know how long it will take. If they've been in there for two months, the mural has had time to affect them." Her eyes, dead serious, fixed on mine. "They have to have the trigger with them at all times. You can't risk that they'll forget again."

I took a long gulp of tea to wet my dry throat. "And so…I can open up a door to the mural from anywhere?"

"You can, but like I said, it's easier to access if you're right in front of it." She got to her feet and came over to brush her hand over my hair. "And I'm going to come with you. I'll help you any way I can."

The pager clipped to her belt vibrated. "I have to call the hospital. Be right back." She went out into the hall. I heard her talking on the phone in surprised tones.

After a couple minutes, she reappeared in the doorway. "One of my patients has just been taken into emergency surgery. They need me at the hospital."

"You can't go now. You just got home. Can't someone cover for you?"

"Sorry, Jules. We're short-staffed as it is. But we'll go as soon as I get back, I promise."

My bottom lip quivered. "I have to know if he's alive, Aunt Karen."

"I know." She gripped me with hands that were as cold as my own. "Don't do anything without me. I'll come home as soon as I can, and we'll go face this together. Just try to keep calm, okay?"

Easy for you to say. I watched her hurry from the kitchen, a shiver running through me.

Once she was gone, I went upstairs to take a shower. I stood under the hot spray, letting it beat down on my head and body. When I got out, some warmth had returned to my extremities, but my insides were still cold with dread.

After I was dressed again, I paced in front of my bed, chewing on my lip. I didn't know how long Aunt Karen was going to be, but I wanted to be ready when she got back. And that meant finding a memory trigger for Nick.

It didn't take me long to think of one.

I took out Mom's album and located the picture of me, Mom and Nick on the night of the junior high graduation. This time when I looked at it, something like hope bubbled up inside of me, nudging aside the dark shadows of grief.

My attention shifted to the centre of the photo, where the locket hung around my neck, its heart-shaped pendent resting just above the neckline of my dress. The silver chain glinted in the June sun.

With an ache rising in my throat, I quickly tucked the photograph into my jeans' pocket. All this time I'd been under the spell of that locket and never known. Now I understood why Mom had given it to me — and why I'd never wanted to take it off. But the idea that my feelings had been manipulated for so long made my skin crawl.

Don't think about that now. Just focus on Nick.

I hoped against hope that he had his wallet in his pocket when he went into the mural. I'd given it to him last Valentine's Day, the day we had the house all to ourselves.

After we exchanged gifts, we'd fallen into an embrace — an embrace that had grown heated as our kisses deepened. Eventually articles of clothing came off, and he laid me back on the sofa. But when he paused with his hand tangled in my dishevelled hair and asked me if I was sure I wanted to keep going, I'd hesitated. That'd been enough to make him stop.

At the time, I had been relieved because I *was* scared to go all the way. I wanted to wait. Since the fire, I'd regretted my decision. If I'd known there wouldn't be another chance for us, I —

My cell phone rang, making me jump a mile. I snatched it up without looking at the caller ID. "Aunt Karen?" I said, breathless.

"No, Julia, it's Jennifer. Jennifer Sampson. We spoke the other day?"

Disappointment coursed through me. "Oh, hi, Jennifer."

"I'm calling because I wanted to keep you in the loop about your mural. I know I told you it wasn't going to be painted over until next week, but there's been a change in plans."

"What do you mean?"

"Well, the head judge, Mr. Marsten, has some family business to attend to next week, so he wants to move up the contest date, which means your mural is going be painted over sooner than we expected, to make way for the new one."

I swallowed. "How much sooner?"

"Well, it depends on the weather, but it looks like it'll be tomorrow or the next day."

In the blink of an eye, the disappointment turned to panic. It clawed at my throat in the form of a barely stifled scream. "No," I gasped. "That's *way* too soon. Please—"

"I'm sorry, dear. But at least you still have a chance to go visit it one last time. I don't mean to cut this short, but I've got another call coming in. Thanks again for giving the city such a beautiful painting."

"But, Jennifer—"

"Bye, Julia." She hung up.

I stared at the phone, stunned that she'd been so determined to get rid of me. But that was the least of my problems. Dread quivered in my belly. In the next couple of days, the mural would be gone–and Nick with it. We had to go in there *now.*

My hands trembled as I called the hospital's surgical ward. When I asked the nurse if my aunt had left the hospital yet, she told me Karen wasn't expected to be out of surgery for a couple more hours.

My heart plummeted. What if a couple hours turned into several? Or my aunt got out of surgery then got pulled onto another case? That kind of thing happened enough for me to know that it was a definite possibility.

By the time she got home, it could be morning—and it might be too late for Nick.

Suddenly every second counted.

With the dread turning into adrenaline that pumped furiously through my veins, I called Luke.

"Well, Princess," he said when he answered, "I've waited long enough. What's the deal? You ready to bring my old man back yet or what?"

I'd waited long enough, too. If Nick had survived, I was ready to do whatever it took to bring him home before the mural was gone forever.

"Yeah," I replied, my voice sounding a lot steadier than I felt. "I need you to pick me up right now. We're going back to the mural. Oh, and, Luke? Bring something that belonged to your father."

* * * *

Less than an hour later, we stood in front of the mural. The evening sun played over the cottages, giving their red and brown façades a soft golden glow. The fir trees stood out in sharp definition, their silver-green branches sparkling like diamonds. And all throughout the painting, the pure white snow glistened wherever it lay—draped over gently sloping hills, cutting swathes around the buildings or wrapped around the outlying mountains like a shimmery veil.

"So," Luke said, eyebrows raised, "do your little magic."

In the car ride over, I'd briefly explained what my aunt had told me about doorways into paintings and what I needed to do. But we'd arrived at the wall before I'd gotten a chance to explain what Luke's role was going to be. He was the last person I wanted as a wingman, but I didn't have much choice.

"I will," I said. Now that I was here, facing what was essentially my door to another realm, my voice did falter a little. "I'm going to go in there and send them back out when I'm sure they remember who they are. I need you to stay here and wait for me, no matter how long it takes."

He turned his blue eyes on me, sceptical. "You want me to wait here the whole time?"

"Just make sure no one's hanging around to see the mural open. If anyone comes along, make something up and get them out of here."

"Fine," he said, taking his lighter and a pack of cigarettes from the pocket of his leather jacket. "And *you* just make sure you bring the old man out in one piece."

I felt inside my pocket for the photograph, then fingered the military dog tags that hung around my neck. According to Luke, his dad had worn them when he served with the Canadian Armed Forces in Afghanistan.

"By the way," I said, "Aunt Karen didn't know anything about a secret way to get rid of the Vista magic forever."

Luke looked at me for several seconds without saying anything, his expression inscrutable. "Well, your mom found a way. And the sooner you get my dad out, the sooner I'll tell you what it is."

I narrowed my eyes at him. I hoped it was true, that there really was a way to get rid of this crazy ability without bottling up my emotions, but I'd have to think about that later. Finding Nick was the most important thing right now.

"Okay, here goes nothing." Taking a deep breath, I faced the mural.

"You need help with the emotional crap again?" Having lit up, he pocketed the lighter and cigarettes and smirked at me.

"Ha ha. I think I can manage on my own, thanks. No locket to hold back my emotions anymore," I added in a mutter.

"Locket?"

I sighed. I hadn't really wanted to get into it. "Yeah. The silver heart I used to wear before I lost it. It's what was blocking my feelings."

"Huh... Weird."

"Now stand back, unless you want to get sucked in, too. Actually, better yet, go on up the street, just to be safe."

"Whatever," he said, blowing out a ring of smoke that sent me into a coughing fit. I waved a hand in front of my face, glaring at him as he walked away.

Then I closed my eyes and began to focus on the emotions swirling inside of me.

"Hey, Princess," Luke called.

I opened my eyes. "What the hell, Luke! You need to be quiet."

He stood about fifteen feet away, his eyes narrowed at me. "I don't think so. Last time pissing you off got the job done quickly—or it would've if your aunt hadn't called. So, while I'm sure it'd be fascinating to watch you do this on your own, I think it works better if I call the shots." He flicked his cigarette on the sidewalk, ground it under the heel of his boot and smiled that cool smile of his. "Let's talk about your mother."

"Luke," I said in a warning voice.

"No, no… This will be good, a quick way to get you going. I want to tell you how she looked in the fire. I mean, it was nasty. Her hair was all singed and her skin had blisters. She had like flames literally burning through her shirt. And her face, oh man, it was all twisted and red. She looked kinda like a monster, you know?"

"You're making that up."

He shrugged. "Does it matter if I am? You're getting pissed off, aren't you? And don't tell me you haven't imagined it before. You must've thought about it over and over, picturing the pain she went through. Am I right?"

"Shut up. Just shut up!"

"What do you think was worse, the pain she felt as she burned to death…or how Nick felt when he realized he wasn't in Kansas anymore?"

"Stop it!" I yelled, clamping my hands to my ears.

"Oh, you're going to hear this. I want to ask you something else. What're you going to do if you get in that mural only to find that Loverboy didn't survive?"

My head pounded. Waves of red-hot anger rolled through me. I hated Luke for being in my house that day. I wanted him to go away so I could find Nick. The emotion crested over me, strong and suffocating.

My eyes closed of their own volition.

The warmth of the autumn sun faded and the air grew chill. A biting wind stung my face. My head drummed with pain and a loud whooshing sound assaulted my ears.

When I was able to open my eyes again, my mural was shimmering.

It shimmered like the bubble in my room, only this one was much wider, running the full length of the mural, and it was even brighter. The colours of the paints moved in a frenzied dance that burned my eyes. Then they stopped moving, and I was looking through a window to the village I'd created.

My painting had come to life…and so had the vortex that wanted to pull me into it. It was even stronger than the one in my room, knocking the wind out of me and carrying me up into a dizzying whirlpool. I tumbled through the air, faster and faster, tossed like a rag doll in a washing machine.

And an instant later, I was inside the mural.

Chapter Six

When I stopped tumbling, I hit something hard. I blinked rapidly as I tried to focus on the surface below my feet.

And let out a gasp. I'd landed on the top of a cottage, of all places.

I flailed on the ice-covered rooftop, my stance awkward on the sloping surface. I reached out for the chimney that lay a couple of feet to my right but lost my balance. I fell on my butt, landing hard on the icy shingles. With nothing to grab onto, I slid down and pitched forward off the roof. A bank of snow helped cushion my fall, but I still came down on my side...hard. Pain shot up my ribs. I lay there for a minute or two, my breaths shallow, a cold wind chilling my body. I half-expected someone to come running out of the cottage, alarmed by the thud on their roof, but nobody showed.

As I finally summoned the strength to sit up, a panicked voice rang through the air. A male voice.

Nick?

I cocked my head, listening. The calls came from somewhere on the other side of a thin stand of fir trees just a few yards away.

My head throbbed and my side burned, but I struggled to my feet. I took a ragged breath and the pain intensified. Lines of black wavered before my eyes. I shook my head until they disappeared, then began to wade through the blanket of pure white snow that stretched around me in every direction.

Soft, pillowy landing spots everywhere and I had to end up on a friggin' roof.

I stumbled towards the voice, moving through the pain, clinging to the hope that Nick was on the other side of the trees. With a hand pressed to my side, I nudged my way through them, their bright green branches stirring in the breeze.

"Help!" the voice called.

My heart sank. That wasn't Nick.

As disappointment coursed through me, I stepped past the trees and onto the bank of a frozen river...frozen except for the jagged opening where a head bobbed up and down.

It was Luke.

Idiot. He should've listened to me about staying back instead of goading me.

"For Christ's sake, help me!"

Luke's reddened fingers curled over the edge of the hole in the ice, but his hands were starting to slip. Immersed in that ice-cold water, he wouldn't be able to hold on for much longer.

"I'm coming. Hang on!" I scanned my surroundings and spotted a tree branch lying on the ground farther down the bank. It hurt to move—hell, it hurt to breathe—but I scooped up the branch and cautiously stepped onto the ice. I began sliding towards Luke. When I was about halfway to the hole, I heard a loud crack. I looked down in horror as a long line split the ice between my feet. I skidded backwards and scrambled back up on the bank, where I collapsed on the hard, cold ground.

Luke flailed in the water, his cries hoarse now. His face had turned a sickly blue.

"Help! Help!" I screamed the word and over, even though I had no idea if anyone was alive in this place.

What seemed an hour later but was probably only a minute, a deep voice drifted towards us, followed by the sound of footsteps crunching on the snow. A man appeared beside me, dressed in a blue coat and matching hat that sparkled like no coat and hat should. "Good God!" he said.

"Please help him," I panted. "I couldn't pull him out. The ice is cracking."

"Hold on, son!" he called to Luke. "I'm going to get a rope." He sprinted away, and I could only stare, helpless, as the bottom half of Luke's face disappeared beneath the water, then reappeared again as he fought to stay afloat, coughing and sputtering.

"Hang on, Luke. Just hang on a little longer!"

While I waited, my teeth chattering, his head slipped underwater several more times as exhaustion set in and the frigid water seeped into his body.

The man crashed through the trees, a long, thick rope in his hands and two younger men in tow. Their clothes shimmered as brightly as the first man's.

"I'll go, Dad. I'm lighter." One of the young men, tall and lean, grabbed the rope and tied it around his waist. Then he lay flat on his stomach on the ice. He inched towards Luke while the two others held onto the other end of the rope, their feet planted firmly on the riverbank.

I held my breath as the young man slithered on the ice. I was sure the crack would widen and he'd join Luke in the water. But his movements were slow and careful, and he reached Luke without incident.

He caught hold of Luke's arms. The two men on the riverbank pulled them both across the ice, which started to splinter again under their combined weight. Frantic now, I stood behind the men, taking a firm grip on the rope myself and pulling with all my might, even though it hurt like hell. With the ice heaving and groaning in protest, we hauled Luke and the young man onto the bank, where they both collapsed.

I knelt over Luke. He lay sprawled on the ground, shivering violently. "You're okay now," I said.

Although his lips moved, no sound came out. He looked up at me, his eyes glassy.

The older man put one arm under his back, the other under his knees and hoisted him against his chest. "Do you live nearby? We need to get him out of these wet clothes right away."

"N-no," I stammered. "We're just passing through. We don't have a place to stay."

He glanced at me curiously. "Well, my cottage is just past the church. We'll take him there."

As he began to cut through the trees, I glanced back at the river—the river that I'd painted, my brush smearing silvery-white tones across the wall that was my canvas. Another chill swept through me...one that had nothing to do with the cold.

* * * *

Something was wrapped snugly around my body. My feet lay in a cocoon of heavenly warmth. A soft pillow cradled my head, easing the ache. The pain in my ribs had abated slightly, now that I was lying still, but they felt constricted. I was groggy, my throat dry and scratchy.

Footsteps approached, and I forced my eyes to stay open. A woman appeared, crouching so she was at eye level with me. I caught the scent of cinnamon and pine. She was in her forties and had a round, kind face with eyes that crinkled at the corners. Her skin was strangely luminescent, and her hair framed her face with curls as red as the poppies in the van Gogh painting. She wore a green dress that matched her emerald eyes. Those eyes focused on me now, dazzlingly bright. I knew her from somewhere—knew her well, actually. So why couldn't I remember *how* I knew her?

"How are you feeling?" she asked.

I rubbed my face, still reeling from the fact that I was not only in my mural, but in one of the cottages. During the short trip from the river, the two young men had held me steady on either side, while the older man had carried Luke like he was as light as a feather. Breathless and in pain, I'd barely noticed my surroundings, other than to marvel at the brilliant colours that coated everything.

The woman had taken our unexpected arrival in stride, first instructing the older man, who turned out to be her husband, to take Luke into a bedroom. She guided me to a small living room, where she settled me on a couch, cinched warm blankets around me and covered my feet with a hot water bottle. I had fallen asleep almost immediately.

"I'm…tired," I said now, in answer to her question.

"I'm not surprised." She patted my hand. "My name is Susan, by the way. And you are…?"

"Julia."

"Nice to meet you, Julia." She smiled, her rosy red lips peeling back to reveal a set of blindingly white teeth. "Seems you've had quite the adventure — and a bit of a shock. But you're safe now. Thank goodness my Gregory found you in time." She smoothed my hair back from my forehead.

Her motherly touch reminded me of Karen. At the thought of my aunt, I was stabbed by a pang of guilt. I wondered if she'd gotten out of the hospital by now. If she had, she would know I'd gone into the mural without her. In Luke's car, I'd dashed off a short text explaining that I couldn't wait.

I focused on Susan again. Suddenly I knew who she was — one of the first villagers I painted. I'd put her on her cottage stoop, her curls peeking out from under a soft blue hat, her cheeks apple-red from the cold and a warm smile lighting up her green eyes.

And now she sat in front of me, no longer just a figure in a mural but a living, breathing person. My heart gave a stutter.

"What is it, Julia?"

"Nothing," I said quickly. "I guess I *am* still in shock. Um, how long was I asleep?"

"A few hours."

"And Luke? Is he okay?"

"He has a mild case of hypothermia, but he'll be just fine. He's still sleeping." She shook her head, her red curls bouncing. "It's a good thing Gregory and my sons got there when they did. It could have been much worse." She paused and peered at me curiously. "What happened out there? How did he fall in the ice? And how did you get hurt? The way you were holding your side when you came in, it looks like you may have bruised your ribs. My son moved the same way when it happened to him."

I fiddled with the edge of the blanket, which shimmered in rich tones of blue and gold. My black sweater looked dull and washed out in comparison. "We, um, didn't know the river wasn't completely frozen solid." I knew it was a lame explanation, so I hurried on before she could press me. "Anyway, I have to go. I need to find someone." With a grimace, I struggled to sit up.

She laid a hand on my arm. "You're hurt."

"It doesn't matter. I have to go."

"I don't think so, dear," she said with a sympathetic smile. "You need to rest before you do anything."

"You don't understand." My head throbbed again and panic speared me like an arrow. I couldn't lie there doing nothing, not when Nick might be in the village. I had to look for him.

Susan shook her head again. "I don't recommend moving around just now. You'll aggravate your injury."

I stared at her. Her hand on my arm was solid. She watched me with her bright green eyes, reminding me of a cat. She was as alive as I was, but she couldn't be real. *Could she?* None of this was real.

"You're *not* real," I whispered.

She blinked. "Excuse me?"

"What's the name of your town?"

"It doesn't have a name," she said, as if this were the most normal thing in the world. "We've just always called it the village."

"And have you ever left the village?"

"Heavens, no." She laughed like it was the funniest thing she'd ever heard. "Why would I do that? This is my home. It's all I've ever known."

Of course it is. Because I made you. I plucked at the blanket and laughed along with her. But I wasn't amused like Susan. I was laughing at the absurdity of it all.

"Yes, my dear, you certainly are in shock. Let me get you some tea to help soothe your nerves."

Yeah, she was a lot like my aunt. I wondered if subconsciously I'd been thinking about Aunt Karen when I had painted Susan.

My hostess was looking at me expectantly. A hot drink actually did sound good before I went back out into the cold. In my haste to get into mural-land, I hadn't thought to bring so much as a pair of gloves. "Okay, fine. One cup before I go."

Susan's animated expression returned as she got to her feet. "Coming right up."

"Hey," I said. "You got anything strong to put in that tea? Um, you know, to help with those nerves."

She thought for a moment, head tilted to one side. "Oh, you know what? I think I do have a bottle of whiskey tucked away. It has great warming and medicinal properties."

As she busied herself in the adjoining kitchen, I examined my surroundings for the first time. The living area was small but cosy. In addition to the couch I was lying on, there was a pair of maroon wingback chairs that flanked a glossy wood coffee table. A stone fireplace was set against one wall. A fire crackled in the hearth, shooting up sparks as bright as shining stars. I stared at it, mesmerized, and felt myself being pulled into sleep again.

The flames rose all around me as the house on Ennis Avenue burned.

"Nick!" I screamed. "Where are you?"

"Upstairs...hurry." His voice was faint in the midst of the roaring inferno. I climbed the steps, tried to take them two at a time, but my ribs ached and it took ages to reach the top.

"Hurry...hurry."

I staggered in the direction of his voice, following it to Mom's bedroom. When I got there, I faced a thick wall of smoke. "Nick! I can't see you."

"I'm over here, honey," came Mom's voice.

The smoke cleared, and I saw her floating above her bed, her body fading in and out. Her hair, so like my own, hung down in a dark curtain. "I'm sorry I didn't tell you about Vistas," she said. "But at least you got to live some of your life normally. Please don't hate me."

"I don't hate you, Mom. I just don't understand what to do here!"

"Don't worry. You'll figure it out." Her voice was fainter now, and so was she. I could barely see the outlines of her body. "Now go. Save Nick. I couldn't do it, but you can."

"But where is he?" I asked, frantic.

"Right here, Julia," said a voice.

I spun around, but there was no one there. I stumbled forward and tripped over something soft and squishy. Bending down, my hand closed over the object — a teddy bear streaked with soot. Its black eyes were hard and unblinking, but its mouth twisted in an evil grin. "You forgot all about me, but I'm right here."

"Julia." A hand shook my shoulder. "Wake up."

"Huh?" I slowly crawled out of the fog of my dream and looked around. Susan squatted in front of me, her eyes pooled with concern.

"You were dreaming."

I blinked at her. She had to be part of my dream, too, didn't she? But I was awake now, and this woman — the one I'd painted on the cottage stoop — placed a comforting hand on my arm, reminding me that she was real. All of this was real.

Susan folded back the covers. "Drink your tea. It will help."

"Ah...yeah. Okay."

She helped ease me to a sitting position. I winced and pressed shaking fingers to my flushed cheeks, the fiery images of the dream still imprinted on my mind. The sense of urgency I'd experienced in my dream mirrored the one I felt in real life. *Nick, where are you?*

When Susan handed me the cup and saucer, it rattled violently. It took a sheer force of will to steady my hands. I took a sip. The tea coated my throat like caramel, warmed my still-cold insides and, after a few moments, took the edge off the pain.

Susan sat across from me, watching as I drank. "There... Isn't that better? I really do think tea is the answer to everything."

"It's good. Thanks." I wrapped my hands around the cup and let the warmth of the ceramic seep into my fingers. "Listen... You said you've never left the village."

"That's right. No one has."

"But has anyone new ever come into the village? Like, recently?"

"Well, you and your friend." She smiled pleasantly.

I bit back my impatience. "Other than us. About two months ago? A man in his fifties and a guy my age?"

"Hmm-m. I don't think so."

The cup and saucer rattled again. "Are you sure? Their names are Nick Allen and Tom Mercer."

"Sorry, dear. I don't know anyone by those names."

"Here," I said, thrusting the cup and saucer at her. Then I fished in my pocket and pulled out the photo taken on the night of the junior high grad. "The guy. Do you recognise him?" I pointed at Nick.

Susan leaned over and peered at the picture. Recognition dawned in her eyes. "Oh my goodness. That looks like a younger version of Daniel."

My throat tightened. I clenched a fold of the blue and gold coverlet, which dazzled my blurred eyes. "Daniel?"

"Yes, but that can't be our Daniel, can it? I don't know where that house is."

"That's the house I grew up in. And that's Nick. He lived across the street from me in a city called St. Peter's."

Susan gave a light chuckle as she got up to take the dishes into the kitchen. "Then it certainly isn't our Daniel. This has always been his home. Strange, though, how much they look alike."

It was him. It had to be. They called him Daniel, which meant he didn't know who he was anymore. But that was okay. I had the picture.

I took a shallow breath. "Where is he? Can you take me to him?"

"Hmm. He's either at his cottage or possibly at the village café now. I can get John or Eddie to go find him."

"I want to go, too. It can't be that far, can it?" Or maybe it was. In my mural, the cluster of cottages were separated from the main buildings by a short trail through the snow, but who knew how the distance translated in real time?

"A five-minute walk, but you really should stay off your feet."

"Please," I begged. "I'll be fine. I just... I need to see him right away. It's important."

She studied me for a long moment, her lips pursed. Finally, she said, "Okay. I'll get John to take you. But go slow," she added. "You still look pale."

"I will."

"And you let your friend stay here and rest. He's definitely not ready to go back out in the cold."

"Yeah, he can just—" I broke off as I felt the blood drain from my face. What if Luke didn't have a memory trigger? He'd been carrying around that cigarette lighter, but I had no idea if that would work or not—or if it had even survived his dunk in the water. "I better check on him before I go."

"Of course."

She helped me up and led me to a small bedroom with cream-coloured walls. The hardwood flooring continued into this room, covered by a brown and green area rug at the foot of the bed. The curtains had been drawn from a window, letting in a shaft of daylight that shone onto the double sleigh bed. There was a wooden rocking chair to one side of the bed. Gregory rose from it when he saw us enter the room.

"How are you, miss?" he said.

"Oh, hanging in there, I guess." I barely glanced at him; my focus was the bed, where Luke lay propped up against a mound of pillows. Wild tufts of hair stood up on his head. His face was a square of white against the deep plum of the top quilt, his lips pale in the light coming from the window. His eyes were half-closed.

"Please, sit," Gregory said, gesturing to the rocking chair. "It might help your friend to see you. He's been disoriented ever since we brought him in."

"Sure, yeah," I said, licking my dry lips. I took my time crossing over to the chair. As I lowered myself onto it, the soreness returned, and I gritted my teeth against it.

"He stopped shivering a while ago," Gregory added, standing at the foot of the bed with his arm slung around his wife. "But he's been muttering off and on and doesn't seem to remember what happened."

"Oh my God."

"Now don't be too alarmed. Confusion is common with even a mild case of hypothermia. It may just take him some time to really come back to us."

I sucked in a breath. *Easy for you to say*. I knew that without a memory trigger, Luke *wouldn't* come back to us.

"Luke?" I said.

His head lolled in the direction of my voice, his eyelids fluttering open. When he didn't answer, I said, "It's me. Julia."

He looked at me with a dazed expression. "Who?" he muttered.

"Julia," I said again, louder.

"Don't know you." He shook his head and winced, as if the movement pained him.

"Do you know your name?" I tried.

Something like recognition broke through the confusion on his face. "Yeah," he said, "I'm…" He stopped, frowning. "I'm not sure." His eyes closed again.

"Gregory," I said sharply. "Where's the leather jacket he was wearing?"

"It's hanging up in the washroom with his other wet clothes."

"I need you to check the pockets for a cigarette lighter. And hurry."

He gave me a quizzical look but didn't question me. When he returned a minute later with the lighter in hand, I heaved a sigh of relief. "Thank God."

"What's this about?" Susan asked.

"Don't worry," I assured her, sitting on the edge of the bed. "We're not going to use it. I just want him to hold it."

Luke's eyes opened when he felt the mattress shift under my weight. "Hold what?"

"Give me your hand."

He slowly withdrew his hand from beneath the mountain of covers. I pressed the lighter against his palm. "Feel that. Look at it. It's yours."

"I don't think so."

"It *is*," I insisted. "See those initials there? LM? Those are yours. Your name is Luke Mercer, and you came here with me. We're here to find your dad."

I waited a long moment as he rubbed his thumb over the initials then turned the lighter over and over in his hand. Finally, he looked up at me. His blue eyes seemed a little more focused, but when he spoke, he said, "Sorry. I don't know what you're talking about."

Don't panic, I commanded myself, even as my stomach gave an uneasy lurch. Maybe he just needed a little more time.

I felt the sudden urge to laugh hysterically, but another glance at Luke's glazed expression sobered me quickly. "Whatever you do, make sure he doesn't let that lighter out of his sight," I said, turning to address Gregory and Susan. "It's important that he sees it. And get him to hold it again, whenever you can."

"Well," Gregory said, scratching his chin, "sure, if you think it's going to help him."

"Thanks. If he asks for me, tell him I'll be back as soon as I can."

And with any luck, I wouldn't be coming back alone.

* * * *

I still couldn't wrap my brain around the fact that I was *in* my mural. It was so surreal to be moving around in something I had created, to see the familiar fir trees swaying in the brisk air, to catch glimpses of the nearby river and the snow-crested mountains in the distance. The cottages were like 3D images on a movie screen, only I didn't need the glasses to get the full effect. The sky was the colour of deep cerulean. I'd finally chosen it after like an hour of waffling between three different shades of blue. Seeing it above me now, shimmering and cloudless, I knew I'd made the right choice. The sun—my sun—shone in that sky, and the powdery white snow sparkled under its abnormally brilliant rays.

John wrapped his arm around my waist to support me as we made our way to the café. He felt as solid and real as his mother, and that boggled my mind, too. He was even less curious about my reason for being there than his mother had been, remaining silent except for the occasional murmur of encouragement.

I didn't walk so much as shuffle through the snow. It hurt to breathe, let alone walk, and every movement made me gasp in pain. But the thought of Nick kept me going. I wouldn't stop until I saw him with my own eyes. And if it was him, really him, I'd get him home.

"Almost there," John said. "How are you doing?"

"Fine," I panted. My head was down as I concentrated on putting one foot in front of the other. I had stopped taking notice of my surroundings, excruciating as it was to move through the pain. But when John spoke again a moment later to tell me we'd arrived, I lifted my head.

And there it was, its big front window glinting in the sun, the deep red of the brick façade vibrant beneath the snow-coated roof. I recognised every detail of it, of course. My hand tingled with the memories of outlining the window with olive green, brushing lemon yellow over the door, and painting the blue-and-white striped awning. Above the awning, with careful strokes, I had spelled out *Village Café* in bold, black letters. Those letters stood out in all their 3D glory.

My breath caught in my throat, and a wave of weakness washed over me. If John hadn't tightened his grip on me, I would have collapsed in the snow.

"Let's get you inside and off your feet," he said.

I nodded, unable to speak.

John opened the door with his free hand and guided me inside. I was instantly engulfed in a sea of warmth that took the edge off my chilled body. A concoction of heavenly aromas reached my nose—rich coffee, hickory bacon and sweet oranges intermingling with the scents of maple, pine and vanilla. I paused just inside the doorway, my breathing shallow, and soaked up the warmth and the smells. I examined the interior of my café. It was everything I'd imagined it would be.

It wasn't a big restaurant, about the size of Aunt Karen's first floor, but it had a high ceiling that gave the impression of roominess. It was crisscrossed with beams the same shade of green as the window trim. The walls were hung with a series of watercolour paintings done in pastel blues, yellows and pinks. Six square tables were arranged in a zig zag pattern, their wooden chairs tucked in neatly. A thick cream-coloured candle sat in the centre of each table, encircled by a plain silver holder. A small counter stood at the rear of the café, and behind it, a door that I assumed led to the kitchen. There were no customers at the moment, and no one was at the counter.

"Café just opened," John explained. "Daniel must be in the back."

My heart pounded in my ears and my palms grew slick with sweat as John helped me over to a table. I lowered myself into a chair.

"You okay? Do you want anything? Water? Coffee?"

"No," I managed. "Just…"

He smiled with understanding. "You just want to see him. I'll be right back."

I watched him walk around the counter like he'd done it a time or two. He disappeared through the door at the back.

Anxious knots twisted in my belly. It was happening. In just a minute, Nick would be there. I'd see his face again, a face I thought would only come to me in dreams for the rest of my life. While everyone had assumed that he was dead, he'd been stuck in the mural for two months, unable to get home. Guilt stabbed at me again. I swore that if we got back to St. Peter's in one piece, I'd never let him out of my sight again.

I waited for the door to the kitchen to swing open, my laboured breathing the only sound in the café. But the minutes ticked by, and the door didn't move.

With a groan, I rested my head in my hands.

Then, finally, I heard the door open. I raised my head. Through the tangles of hair hanging in my face, I saw a tall figure standing behind the counter.

"Hello?"

I pushed my hair behind my ears…and stared.

Chapter Seven

His hair was longer than I remembered, falling over his forehead in a wave of chestnut brown, and uncharacteristic stubble dusted his cheeks — but it was definitely Nick. It was his square-cut jaw, his wide, expressive mouth, and eyes the colour of golden caramel. Those eyes stared at me from across the room, widened in confusion. I stared back, drinking in every detail of his face.

This is it. Any second now I'm going to wake up and find it's another dream. He's not real.

"Nick?" I said in disbelief.

He stepped around the counter and began striding across the café towards me. I put my hands flat on the table and pushed myself up with a strength I didn't know I had. When there were still several feet between us, he stopped. He pursed his mouth for a second, then said, "No, my name is Daniel."

My chest tightened. If I hadn't been able to breathe before, I really couldn't now. I stumbled against the chair.

"Take it easy," he said, closing the gap between us. He placed his hands on my shoulders, steadying me. At his touch, a million goosebumps rose on my skin. I looked up at him, and his eyes locked onto mine.

I itched to run my fingers through his hair, to touch his face. I needed to make sure he was real and not just a figment of my imagination. But I hesitated, afraid that if I did, he would vanish into thin air.

"Are you real?" I asked.

His mouth curved slightly, giving me just a taste of that crooked smile I knew so well…and launching my heart into overdrive. "I'd like to think so."

"You seem real," I said. "Please don't disappear."

He raised his eyebrows, his smile fading. "Ah, okay. Hey, why don't you sit down?"

I shook my head. "No, I need to look at you." I raised my hand and traced his jawline with a trembling finger. When he didn't evaporate, I smoothed his hair back from his forehead. I swallowed the lump in my throat and whispered, "It *is* you."

Then, unable to hold back any longer, I threw my arms around him and buried my face in his chest. He was warm and solid, his breath tickling my ear. Just the closeness of him sent little currents of electricity through me. He was flesh and bone, smelling like soap and pine. The ache in my ribs faded into the background as I stood clasping him.

My heart thudded so loudly in my chest that I was sure he could hear it. For the first time since I'd lost my locket, I felt the dark emotions start to lift.

Nick is alive.

He patted my back and gently peeled my arms from around his neck as he let out an awkward laugh. "I'm not who you think I am. You've mistaken me for someone else."

"No, I haven't," I said firmly. "You're not Daniel. You just think you are. Your name is Nick. Nick Allen."

He rubbed his cheek. "Never heard that name in my life."

"I'm Julia," I persisted, "your girlfriend."

He searched my face. I dug my fingernails into my palms as I waited for some sign of recognition. But his gaze remained blank, and my heart sank all the way down to my toes.

"Sorry," he said. "You have the wrong guy. I honestly don't think we've ever met."

"You were in a fire." My voice shook, and I struggled to keep it steady. "I-I thought you were dead."

"Look," he said. "John told me you took a knock to the ribs. You've obviously been through a lot and you're not thinking straight. Just—"

"No!" With frustration bubbling up inside me, I yanked the photograph from my pocket. "I *am* thinking straight. I know exactly who you are, and you do, too. You just have to concentrate. Look at this picture."

A wary expression crossed his face, but he took the picture from me. He studied it for a few seconds. Then he turned his attention back to me, his eyes round with shock. "What the—?"

"That's *you*, Nick. You and me and my mother. That was the night of our junior high graduation." I grabbed his hand and squeezed it. "Don't you see? You were sent here by mistake. You don't belong here."

He glanced from me to the picture and back again. "It's not possible. I don't remember this."

"Just give it a minute. It'll come back to you." I sucked in a breath, hoping against hope that it *would* come back to him. Because if it didn't... Well, I didn't want to think about that right now.

"Aren't you going to introduce me to your friend, Daniel?" a voice asked from behind us.

Nick pulled his hand from mine and quickly stepped back from me. His eyes shifted guiltily away and colour flooded his pale cheeks. Annoyed at being interrupted, I turned to see a young woman standing in the doorway next to John. She had an hourglass figure and skin the colour of ivory. Her apple-red hair fell around her shoulders in sleek, tidy waves. She had a sharp, angular face and high cheekbones that looked like they could have been sculpted from porcelain. She lifted her glossy red lips in a bright, insincere smile. The suspicion in her eyes was unmistakable.

"Well, Daniel?" she demanded, addressing Nick, even as she gaped at me. "Who *is* this?"

"Julia," I supplied before he could answer. "I'm his girlfriend."

She let out a haughty laugh. "I don't think so. He would never be with anyone so" — she wrinkled her nose — "plain."

"Stacey!" John exclaimed.

"What?" she shrugged, the picture of innocence. "You know you were thinking it, too."

I took several deep breaths. *Don't let her get to you.* "Listen, ah...Stacey, is it?" I plastered a smile on my face that I'm sure looked every bit as fake as hers. "I need to talk to N—Daniel in private. So why don't you—?"

"No," she interrupted. "Anything you have to say to him, you can say in front of me. Right, Daniel?"

Nick—who'd been watching the exchange with obvious discomfort—cleared his throat. He glanced down at the picture again. "Just give us a few minutes, Stacey."

"Excuse me?" Stacey said loudly. "What's going on here? You're not seriously telling me you know this girl?"

"I'm not sure." Nick raked his fingers through his hair. "Just go. Please."

Thank God. His memory might not have returned yet, but the picture had triggered *something* in him. At least he was willing to talk to me.

The door to the café opened and in stepped a stout woman with hair the same colour as Stacey's. She was plump where Stacey was slender, her complexion rosy instead of bone white. When her eyes settled on me, she gave me a warm smile. "Well, hello, dear. So nice to see a new face in the village. We don't get many visitors. And who might you be?"

"This is Julia," Nick piped up, giving me an uneasy smile.

"She just barged in here where she doesn't belong," Stacey said, flashing daggers my way. "You have to do something, Mom."

The woman frowned. "Don't cause trouble, Stacey. You know anyone is welcome in my café."

"Daniel wants to talk to Julia alone, but Stacey is being…difficult." This from John, who I was really starting to like.

"Stacey," the woman said in a warning voice, "go in the kitchen with John."

"But, Mom—"

"Go. *Now*."

Stacey sent me one last withering look before following John into the other room.

Stacey's mother approached me, peeling off her gloves. "I'm pleased to meet you, Julia. I'm Doris Clifton." She extended a hand for me to shake, then frowned as her warm fingers clasped my cold ones. "My dear, you feel like an icicle. And you don't look well. You need to sit down. Here."

As she held out the chair for me, I sat down cautiously, bracing myself for another jolt to my ribs.

Doris peered at me in concern. "Are you sick?"

"No," I said. "I hurt my ribs."

She clucked her tongue. "Then you shouldn't be out and about. Why aren't you resting?"

"Because it's really important that I talk to Nic…ah, Daniel."

"Nonsense. You're pale and obviously weak."

And I desperately wanted to lay my head on the table and close my eyes, but I fought the urge. There'd be plenty of time for rest later, when Nick was himself again and we were home. Before I could voice another protest, Nick spoke up.

"Doris is right. You should be taking it easy. But…you're right, too." His gaze rested on my face. The familiar warmth of his eyes tugged at my heartstrings. "I'll take you to my cottage. We can talk there, and you can rest at the same time."

"All right," I agreed. I knew I'd have to get back to Luke soon, and we had to find Tom…but at that moment, all I cared about was being with Nick.

"Well," Doris said, pleased, "that sounds like a sensible plan. Let me wrap up some food for you to take with you."

"It's not far," Nick said when Doris had disappeared into the kitchen. "And there won't be any interruptions there." His eyes gravitated to the picture again. There were questions written all over his face.

"It might help if you keep that photo with you," I said.

He frowned at me a little but tucked the picture into the pocket of his shirt.

Doris bustled out of the kitchen with a large brown paper bag. Then Nick was next to me, helping me up and out of the café. I smiled sleepily, relishing the feel of his arm around my waist. As he bundled me into some kind of sleigh, tucking a bright red blanket around me, I murmured, "I can't believe you're here."

He didn't reply, just jumped up onto the front seat and lightly snapped the reins. The horse, a dapple grey, started to move. The runners of the sleigh made a swishing sound as they slid through the snow. Clusters of cottages passed by on either side of me, interspersed with forested slopes. Trees drifted past, their velvety green branches glittering with frost, their trunks the colour of rich cocoa. The icy peaks of the mountains shimmered in the distance.

I closed my eyes, my stomach churning.

It was just too surreal. I couldn't really be in my mural, could I? When I opened my eyes again, the glistening landscape would be gone. I'd find that this was all a dream.

"Are you all right back there?"

I opened my eyes. If it was a dream, then why did Nick seem so real? He peered over his shoulder at me, his eyebrows raised.

I swallowed, my throat as dry as cotton balls. My ribs were killing me, but he didn't need to know that. "Yeah, I'm fine."

"Hold on a little bit longer. We're almost there."

"Okay. Good." I licked my lips. "Nick —"

"Daniel," he corrected.

"You really don't remember how you got here?"

He frowned. "I've always been here."

"That picture in your pocket tells a different story, though, doesn't it?"

"I don't understand it. It doesn't make sense." He faced forward, his shoulders set in a rigid line. "And I want you to explain it to me after the doctor checks you out."

"Doctor?" I gaped at him.

"You say you're fine, but you're obviously not. Don't worry. He happens to live close by. I'm going to get him once I get you settled."

"But I don't need —"

"Here it is," he interrupted. "Told you it wasn't far."

We entered a clearing, and a small cabin came into view. The building had logs the colour of maple syrup and a gable roof layered with snow. A stone chimney poked up on one side. Piles of chopped wood were stacked at various points along a wraparound porch. On the front of the cabin, two curtained windows flanked a solid oak door.

Nick stopped the sleigh, hopped down and tied the reins to a post. Then he turned and, putting an arm around me, helped me down. I grunted from the pressure on my ribs and staggered as my feet hit the ground. I careened into him. He caught me neatly in his arms, steadying me. We were face-to-face, so close our

Captured in Paint

mouths almost touched. My breath caught in my throat.

The warm brown pools of his eyes gazed into mine. They definitely looked too real to be part of a dream. How was it possible that for two months he'd been lost to me forever, and now he was with me — solid, warm and alive? My hand moved of its own volition and I brushed his cheek. I was overcome with the need to have his lips on mine. Those two months without feeling his kiss had felt like two lifetimes.

But just before my lips brushed his, he pulled away, quickly averting his head. An embarrassed flush crept up my neck and spread across my face. For a second there, I'd been lost in his eyes, and the way the soft light picked out the golden flecks in his irises. But I couldn't forget that he didn't know me. As far as he was concerned, I was a complete stranger. The realization struck me in the stomach like a cold fist.

He cleared his throat. "Sorry. I didn't mean to stare."

"No, I shouldn't have touched you like that. It's just...automatic for me, I guess."

"Probably best if you don't do it again." His voice was gentle, but his words cut like a knife. "All this is a lot to take in." He studiously avoided looking at me now, his gaze focused downward as he brushed snow from his pants.

"Right. Yeah. I get it." *It doesn't matter,* I told myself. *I'll fix this. He'll know me soon enough.* But the cold spread upwards from my belly, clamping around my heart like an icy band of steel. I swayed a little, feeling woozy again, and he snapped to attention.

"You're shivering. Come on."

Nick led me into the cottage. It was warm and cosy inside, with a large living area that led into a small

127

kitchen. He strode to a sofa set against one wall, tossed aside the cushions and pulled out a bed, insisting that I lie down while he went to get the doctor.

When the cabin door shut behind him, I propped myself up on my elbows. My gaze darted around the room. A square end table stood on either side of the sofa bed, each one holding a kerosene lamp that cast a glow on the rough-hewn log walls. An overstuffed taupe armchair sat to the left of a flagstone fireplace, while a hickory rocker with a twill plaid cushion took up home on the right. An oval-shaped area rug lay in the centre of the gleaming hardwood floor.

From my spot on the sofa, I had a view of the mountains from the front window. They rose in the distance like a mirage, floating against the cerulean sky in undulating patterns of white and green. I stared for a long moment, transfixed. Those weren't just any mountains. They were *my* mountains. My stomach rolled at the thought.

The door opened, causing me to tear my gaze from the window. Nick entered the cabin, accompanied by a man with coppery hair and rosy cheeks. He smiled when he saw me. His eyes were the colour of golden-brown sand.

He didn't look familiar, so I figured he must've been one of a group of villagers I'd painted. He blended in with the rest in my mind. I had no idea how he'd become the village's resident doctor, but several of the people here seemed to take on roles and personalities that I'd never imagined.

"Hello there," he said in a deep, friendly voice.

Nick quickly made the introductions. "Julia, this is Dr. Evans. Dr. Evans, Julia. She's —"

"Just visiting," I interjected.

"Visiting? Well now, I can't remember the last time we had someone new in the village, if ever!" He chuckled. "Can you, Nick?"

Nick frowned. "No, I can't."

I wanted to tear out my hair in frustration. How could he say that? *He* was new. And what was the deal with this doctor and the other residents not remembering when Nick had first appeared in the village? Were they all under the same spell as he was, believing he'd always been one of them?

"No matter," the doctor continued. "Nick tells me your ribs are sore."

"Yeah, I fell."

"Let me take a look."

He examined me, pressed gently on my ribs — it was all I could do not to gasp — and asked me a few questions. Then he nodded. "Uh-huh. Just as I suspected. Your ribs aren't broken, just bruised." He patted the black bag he'd laid on the table. "I brought a bottle of apple cider vinegar with me. It does wonders for bruises. I'll make you up a compress for you to put on those ribs now, and Nick can change it for you in a couple of hours. How does that sound?"

I let out a strained laugh. "Well, not as good as a couple of aspirin."

Dr. Evans and Nick exchanged a confused look. Okay then. Guess that didn't exist here. *Note to self: add a bottle of pain reliever to next painting.*

"Never mind," I said. "That sounds fine."

After immersing a large piece of cloth in the vinegar, the doctor instructed me to hold it against my ribs. "There," he said. "That should help with the pain. I'm also going to leave Epsom salts and lavender oil for you to soak in later." He turned to Nick. "You need anything else, young man, you just let me know."

"I will."

Dr. Evans treated me to another smile. "You take care now, Julia. And welcome."

"Thanks," I said.

When the doctor was gone, Nick sent me a curious glance before going to the kitchen to flick a dial on the stove. Then he came to stand awkwardly by the bed. "How did you fall?"

"It's not important. Listen…"

I broke off because, at the same time, he said, "I'm sure…"

"You first," I said. Suddenly I felt nervous, which was crazy since I'd known Nick most of my life and had always told him everything. But, I reminded myself, this wasn't exactly Nick.

"I'm sure you'll feel a lot better in a day or two. The doctor really knows what he's doing."

I nodded. Now that I had the floor, I found myself unable to speak. *Where do I start?*

He turned and busied himself at the fireplace, throwing in logs and lighting them with a match. Soon he had a small fire going. He jabbed at the blaze with a poker. The yellow-white flames danced in response, the light playing over his profile.

Turning from the hearth, he pulled the photo from his pocket and held it up. "The guy in this picture looks exactly like me. I want to know why that is."

"Because it is you, Nick."

"My *name* is Daniel!" he said sharply. "And this guy isn't me. He can't be. I was never at this house, and I've never seen this woman — or you — in my life."

I wasn't sure what pained me more — the certainty in his voice or the anger that flared in his eyes.

"So, tell me the truth," he continued, his voice rising several octaves. "What's going on here? I really can't—"

The kettle whistled on the stove, the shrill sound cutting him off mid-sentence. Rubbing his neck, he slipped into the kitchen. I leaned back against the pillows and closed my eyes. It was Nick rustling around in the room next to me, but at the same time, it wasn't. With my breath hitching, I willed myself to stay calm, to bury the frustration that rose inside me.

"Here you go." I opened my eyes. He was moving towards the bed with a mug in his hands. "Drink some tea. It'll warm you up."

Tea again. Of course.

His voice was warm and gentle, and as I reached out to take the mug from him, I was relieved to see that the anger had faded from his eyes. "Thanks."

He sat on the edge of the bed as I took a drink. "I'm sorry about before...for yelling at you like that."

"It's okay," I said, staring down at the mug cradled in my hands. "I know it must be confusing."

"It is." He ran both hands through his hair. "You think I'm this Nick guy. And in the café you said I was sent here. Sent here from *where*, exactly?"

"From St. Peter's. It's a small city on the east coast of Canada."

"But I've never been there. I've never been anywhere but here."

"I know it seems that way, but..." I paused, racking my brain for a way to describe what had happened to him. "It's this place. It's playing tricks on your mind, making you forget everything about your life."

"*This* is my life. Here, in the village."

"Nick," I said, and held up a hand before he could correct me again. "The village is not part of the real world. I... Well, it's a mural I painted. And it's not going to be around for much longer."

"Oh, really? Where is it going?"

"It's being painted over. And we need to get out of here before that happens."

"A mural." He let out a short, humourless laugh. "I think something is playing tricks with *your* mind. And just how do you think I was sent here? Someone waved a magic wand?"

I bit my lip. "My mother opened a portal. You were pulled in."

"A portal," he repeated in a flat voice.

"Right. I come from a family of people who can open these portals. They're like doors into pictures and paintings. Only I didn't know I could open them until recently."

He stared at me for several beats, then in one abrupt movement, got to his feet. He picked up the poker again and prodded the fire logs. I waited for him to say something–anything–but he remained silent as he stood with his back to me, his hands steady on the poker.

Finally, I couldn't take it anymore. "Nick," I said, a pleading note in my voice, "don't you remember me?"

He turned around slowly, the poker still clutched in his hand. "All this talk about portals and me being from this other world... It's just crazy, okay? You must've hit your head or something when you fell. You can stay here tonight and get some rest. But I think it's best for both of us if you leave in the morning."

I took a shallow breath. "But what about the picture?"

"I don't know about that. Must be somebody who looks like me."

"Nick—"

"I told you," he said. His eyes, steady on mine, were devoid of emotion. And that cut more deeply than his anger ever could. "My name is Daniel."

I set the mug on the table beside the bed and tucked my wayward hair behind my ears. "Listen to me, okay? I know I can jog your memory if you just give me a chance to explain. First of all, you were in a fire."

"What? No, I wasn't."

"Please, just hear me out. It was the night of the awards ceremony. You'd won a humanitarian award. The three of us were going together—me, you and Mom. But we never got there because the fire broke out." My throat was beginning to ache, and I swallowed painfully. "You lost consciousness and when Mom opened a door to the mural, you got sucked through it. And I came here to take you back. But I can't do it if you don't remember who you are. Please, try to remember."

"How can I remember something that didn't happen?" He sighed. "Maybe you have a concussion or you're confusing dreams with reality. Or—"

"*No!*" The word burst out of me with such vehemence that he took a step back, startled. "It's all true." The frustration I'd been pushing down suddenly leaped back up, mingling with a fresh onslaught of grief as I relived that night in my mind. "I saw the fire with my own eyes. I thought you were trapped inside. There was a memorial service and everything. Your parents just started a scholarship fund in your name. I've known you since we were kids, Nick. And suddenly, you were just…gone."

He just looked at me like I had two heads.

"Everyone assumed you burned in that fire," I said, my voice wobbling. "But you didn't. And I am so friggin' grateful for that. But still, because of Mom, you ended up here, and I can't imagine what that's been like for you. God, I wish I could go back to that day. Maybe if I'd been there, none of this would've happened. I wouldn't have lost you. We wouldn't have been separated. Mom would still —" I ran out of breath as my ribs kicked up an assault. Hot tears stung my eyes.

"Hey," he said, coming back to the side of the bed, "take it easy. You're getting yourself all worked up again. It's obvious that being around me reminds of you of this guy who looks like me. Just lie back and get some rest. And like I said, in the morning —"

"I'm not leaving in the morning," I said. "I won't lose you again."

He rubbed his temples, as if I were giving him a headache. He didn't remember…and he didn't believe me.

Before I could stop them, tears spilled from my eyes and ran down my flushed cheeks. Frustration and despair washed over me like a river current, fast and strong. With the jumble of emotions overpowering me, I wished I didn't have to go through this. I wished I could take him home *now*.

The dizziness struck me head on. My eyes sealed shut.

Then came a clanging sound so loud it made my ears ring, and I was able to open my eyes.

Nick stared at me, his eyes wide with shock and disbelief. The poker lay at his feet, where he'd dropped it on the hardwood floor. "How did you —?" His head swivelled to the door of the cottage, then whipped back to me again. "There was something glowing over there. What *was* that?"

I struggled for breath for several seconds. That was close. Way too close. I had to get myself under control. "I started to open a door. A door back home."

Now he shook his head as if to clear it. "How did you do that? Is it an illusion?"

"I told you, I can open doors in and out of paintings. When I'm feeling really intense emotions, it just happens. That's how I got to the village, through a portal. It's how *you* got here."

All the blood drained out of his face. He stumbled into the kitchen, took a glass down from a cupboard and filled it up at the sink. I waited while he gulped it down, moving in front of the fire to warm my hands.

When he came to stand next to me a minute later, his breathing sounded as shallow as my own, but a little colour had returned to his cheeks. I looked up into his eyes. They were full of fear and confusion. When he spoke, his voice was hoarse. "I don't want to believe it. I don't want to believe what you just did. But I saw it. I saw *something*."

"I'll tell you everything, okay? I'll tell you about us, about my mom, about your life in St. Peter's. But I need you to listen."

He nodded, his face grim. "All right. I'll listen."

* * * *

The next morning, the sun rose over my mural, streaking the sky with shades of apricot and rose. An ethereal mist pooled over the mountains, suffusing the peaks with a violet glow. As the sun climbed higher, the mist dissipated and the snowy landscape shimmered under golden shafts of light. I stared out of the window, captivated by the surreal scene, a coffee Thermos in my hands.

I'd woken up just minutes earlier to find myself alone in the cottage. There was a note from Nick on the pillow next to me, indicating that he'd gone to feed Dusty, the horse, and that I should help myself to the coffee on the side table.

I swung my legs over the side of the bed. My ribs still throbbed with pain, but it was nowhere near as excruciating as the day before. I couldn't believe the apple cider compresses had actually worked.

I pushed myself up and padded to the kitchen, where I leaned against the counter and took in the view from the back window. The sun swept over the fields and trees, making them glow. A small barn gleamed a rich red in the explosion of dawn. Nick and Dusty stood in front of the open doors. Flurries drifted around them in lazy circles. He brushed the horse's lustrous coat with a gloved hand, his lips moving.

Velvety darkness had fallen by the time I'd finished telling Nick my story. I'd told him everything, starting with how I'd open a portal as a kid, how Luke's father, intent on revenge, had confronted Mom. Nick listened, incredulous, as I explained how Luke had come looking for his father and the fire had broken out, and how Mom had created the door to the mural. Finally, I told him about tumbling into the painting with Luke.

When I finished, Nick raised his eyebrows at me. "That's a crazy story."

"I know how it sounds, but—"

"And you're saying this guy, Tom, this alcoholic, is here, too? I don't know anybody like that."

"I don't know for sure if he's here," I said, holding a compress against my ribs. "But he blames me for the way Luke turned out."

"So your...ability. You really didn't know about it?"

"No. Not until I lost my locket. It was charmed to take away my power. You know the locket," I added. "You teased me for never taking it off." He looked at me with a blank expression. I sighed. "You don't remember that either, huh?"

He leaned forward on the armchair, his elbows propped on his thighs. "No, I don't. And I don't understand why you want me to carry the picture."

I'd done my best to explain how a personal item acted as a memory trigger when someone was inside a painting, but he just seemed even more confused. Even after I'd spent the better part of an hour telling him about our relationship, he still didn't show any signs of recognition. After an awkward silence, he had wished me goodnight and disappeared into the bedroom adjacent to the living area.

It'd taken every ounce of my will not to cry myself to sleep.

Now I watched him tend to the horse. Even from where I stood, I could see his solemn expression. My Nick was inside there somewhere, but I didn't know how to get him out.

I shuffled to the table and sat. Should I go back to Susan's, find out if Luke had fared any better than Nick when it came to regaining his memories? Or should I stay here? I dropped my head in my hands and sat there for I don't know how long, only looking up when Nick stepped into the cabin.

His cheeks were flushed from the cold, his hair damp from the light snow. Dark circles shadowed his eyes, and his mouth stretched in a grim line across his face. He stomped his boots on the mat inside the door and hung his coat on a peg. When he moved toward the kitchen, his expression softened.

"Hey," I said.

"Hey." His arms hung awkwardly at his sides. "Listen… I'm sorry you lost your mom."

"Thanks."

He sat across from me and lifted his clouded eyes to meet mine. "I didn't get much sleep last night, thinking about everything you've told me. And I've looked at the picture" —he patted his pocket—"over and over. But I still can't make sense of any of it."

I hadn't slept well either, knowing he was lying in the next room. So close and yet so far away.

"Do you still think I'm crazy?"

"I don't know. I mean, I've seen what you can do. I just can't remember being in this other place, this St. Peter's. Or being with you."

I bit my lip and stared down at my hands, twisted together on the table to keep them from shaking. "Will you take me to see Luke? I have to check on him. He's still over there at Susan's."

"Yeah, I can do that."

I raised my head and gave him a tight smile. "And who knows? Maybe something about him will jog your memory." *And if I have two guys with amnesia, I'm screwed.*

"I'll make breakfast first. You must be starving. You barely touched Doris' sandwiches last night."

As if on cue, my stomach gave a loud rumble, making me blush.

"And that answers my question." His mouth turned up in his lopsided grin, and I caught the flash of his dimple just before he turned and went into the kitchen. Goosebumps rose on my arms. God, how I'd missed that dimple. I'd missed *him*.

And it was taking everything in my power not to throw my arms around him again.

He served breakfast at the little table—an omelette stuffed with cheese, peppers and onions, strips of crisp bacon, golden hash browns flavoured with savory and fresh, tangy orange juice. I devoured every bite.

"How did you get so good in the kitchen?" I asked, scraping up the last bit of egg with my fork. "Back home you could barely boil a pot of water."

He lifted a shoulder in a half shrug as he picked up our dishes. "I work at Doris' café. She taught me everything I know."

"Huh." I peered at him curiously. It was so weird to think of him having this other life that I knew nothing about. "Do you like working there?"

"I love it. The people are great and Doris is really flexible."

"And what about her daughter? She seemed pretty...demanding."

"Stacey?" He'd turned to put the dishes in the sink, so I couldn't see his expression as he rinsed off the plates. "She's always been a bit protective of me."

"Protective?" I scoffed. "She practically bit my head off."

He swivelled around and gave me a rueful smile. "Yeah, sorry about that. She can be blunt."

More like bitchy. In fact, she reminded me of Trisha. And wasn't it just my luck that there was someone like her in this world, too.

"She does a lot for me, though," Nick continued. "Both her and Doris have."

"So is she a friend…or more than that?" I took a gulp of my juice, dreading the answer.

"She's just a friend, although sometimes I think she wants more than that."

The juice went down the wrong way, stinging my throat. Nick was at my side in a flash, lightly thumping on my back as I coughed. "Are you okay?"

"Fine," I said when I was able to stop sputtering.

He gave me one last pat on the back and stepped back. Anxiety settled in my gut like a rock. "And what about you? Do you want more from her?"

"No, I don't think of her like that. She…well, she's not the kind of person I could see myself in a relationship with."

"Oh." I couldn't help but smile.

His gaze rested on my face for a long moment, and I wondered if he was thinking about what I'd told him about *our* relationship.

A tangle of hair fell in my eyes. I shifted uncomfortably, suddenly feeling clammy and gross in my clothes from the day before.

"Can I get washed up, maybe borrow some clean clothes?"

"How about a bath? The doctor left the Epsom salts and lavender oil for you to soak in."

"Ah, yeah. Okay."

He grabbed the bag of salts and a small bottle of oil from a cupboard, then led me to the bathroom. It was a small but airy room done in creamy whites and rich browns. A claw-foot bathtub sat under a window that overlooked the field.

Nick opened the cabinet below the sink and withdrew a large yellow bath towel. He handed it to me. When he ran the bathwater, he added a generous amount of the salt and lavender oil.

"I'll give you a few minutes to...get ready," he said. "Wrap yourself in the towel."

"Um, what do you mean?"

"I'm going to help you in and out of the tub."

I shook my head. "Uh-uh. No way."

"Your ribs might feel better today, but they're still healing. You need to go slow. You don't want to slip and fall, do you?"

A warm flush crept up my neck. "I think I can manage on my own."

"Don't worry, Julia," he said with a sigh. "I'm not planning on being there for the main event. But you've got to let me help you."

I pressed my fingers to my blazing cheeks. As much as I wanted to be physically close to Nick, the thought of him seeing me sans clothes made me squirm uncomfortably. Now that he was convinced he was this Daniel person, it was almost like he was a stranger. Showing that much skin...? Talk about awkward.

He looked at me with a mix of concern and puzzlement. "What's wrong? I'm serious. I'll be in and out. I just don't want you to get hurt again."

"Fine. But eyes up here," I said, pointing at my face.

"I swear, I'll be the perfect gentleman."

As the bathroom door closed behind him, I stared at the tub, quickly filling up with water, then at the towel in my hand. I sighed. It was now or never. I set the towel down next to the sink and slowly pulled off my clothes. A few minutes later, Nick rapped on the door.

"You ready?"

"Just a second!" I called. Gritting my teeth, I yanked off my socks, then reached for the towel. With

141

trembling hands, I threw it around my shoulders and held it so that the material was taut over my chest and fell below my knees. "Okay, ready now."

He came in, and with barely a glance in my direction, leaned over the tub to turn off the water. I moved so that I was directly behind him. He turned around, startled, bumping my shoulder with his elbow. "Oh, there you are. Sorry."

"It's okay," I said with a nervous laugh. "I won't break that easily."

He smiled shyly, his eyes locked on mine, and there was that electric tension again between us, making my heart gallop.

"So," he said, "all set?"

I cleared my throat. "Sure." I let the towel fall away. True to his word, Nick kept his eyes on my face and his hands on my arms as I stepped into the tub. As soon as I slid down in the water, he turned away. "Just yell if you need anything. I'll be back to get you out in fifteen minutes."

"Okay. Thanks."

Relief poured over me as I heard the door close softly behind him. It was just too much to be close to him like that when he didn't know me.

The warm water felt heavenly and eased the ache in my ribs. I lathered soap on my skin and washed the grit out of my hair. By the time Nick knocked on the door, I was feeling human again.

"I'm ready. Come in."

He entered the room and set some clothes next to the sink. "Let's get you out of there." He extended his arms and I let him help me over the lip of the tub and onto the soft bathmat. I shivered as air hit my skin. Nick snatched the towel and wrapped it around my shoulders. Then he paused, his eyes meeting mine.

"Feel better?"

I nodded. "Much."

"Good." He took a step back, but his gaze didn't waver from my face.

My pulse jumped. Had he remembered something? Had he remembered *me*? "What is it?"

He gave a half laugh. "Well, it's just...you have really pretty eyes. You'd think if I knew you, I would've remembered them."

"Oh." I dug my nails into the soft material of the towel and sucked in a breath. "I know this all sounds crazy. I can see why it's hard to believe. You just need time."

He sighed. "Maybe you do have this magical ability, but the guy you're looking for, it's not me."

My heart sank like an anchor falling to the bottom of the ocean. The tears were threatening to fall again, pricking my eyes. I had to get them under control, and I didn't think I could do it with his eyes locked on me in that penetrating gaze.

"Julia?"

"I can't talk about this right now. Will you please just let me get dressed?"

"All right," he said. "Take your time."

This time when the door shut, I sat on the edge of the tub, barely succeeding in pushing back the wave of emotions before it could wash over me.

* * * *

I emerged from the bathroom and shuffled down the short hallway. Nick glanced up when I entered the living room. Then he went back to folding the sheets and blankets on the sofa bed.

I sat on the edge of the armchair and watched him, unsure of what to say. My towel-dried hair hung in damp waves around my face. I felt refreshed wearing the clean cotton shirt and jeans Nick had laid out, even though they were a bit baggy on me.

The silence stretched out between us, broken only by the creak of the eaves as the wind whistled through them.

I swallowed thickly. "I thought you were dead, you and Mom. I lost my home, my family. And I kinda felt dead too, on the inside. It was like these horrible dark feelings were in there somewhere, but they wouldn't come out. I mean, I've always been pretty good at not getting overwhelmed by feelings, you know that."

Nick didn't say a word, just raised an eyebrow at me. I heaved a sigh. Of course he didn't know.

"Anyway," I continued, "this time I thought I'd be able to cry easily, like my Aunt Karen. But nothing, not even one little tear. I don't know, I guess I figured it was just shock that kept me from losing it." I let out a harsh laugh. "Of course, everyone thought I was this callous bitch because I didn't show any emotion after the fire. I was okay with it, though. It's what got me through each day, not being able to really feel."

I paused. Again, no comment from Nick, but I could tell from the way he kept glancing over that he was listening. And, for now, that would have to be enough. "But when I lost my locket, suddenly I felt like having a meltdown almost every second. I thought it was because that locket was all I had left of Mom and not having it anymore… Well, I guessed everything just hit me all at once."

Nick dropped the folded quilt on the bed and turned to look at me full on. "So then you did cry?"

"Yeah," I said, twisting my hands together in my lap, "because I wasn't protected by the locket anymore. Now, seeing you again after all this time, after thinking you were dead… Well, it's bringing up a lot of strong feelings. I have to get control of them. If I don't, I'll open a door before we're ready to go back."

He crossed the room and sat next to me. "Look…I'm sorry you're dealing with this. And I'll do whatever I can to help you stay calm while you're here. But I'm not going through any magical doors. This is my home."

I took a deep breath but didn't say anything.

"I'll take you back to Luke. I'm sure you guys can figure this all out."

"Right," I said, biting my lip, "Luke." Even though I knew I should check on him, I wanted to stay there with Nick.

"Don't get upset," he said gently. "But I'm not the one you're looking for."

"You *are* the one, Nick." I put my hand over his, pressed it down firmly so he couldn't slide from my grasp.

He drew a sharp intake of breath. His eyes changed, became glassy.

"Nick?"

He shook himself and his eyes cleared. "Sorry."

"Did you remember something?"

"No, I— No." Now he did slip his hand out from under mine. "I'll take you back to Susan's now. Just let me get Dusty ready."

He pulled his coat on and went outside.

Sitting in the quiet of the cabin, I wondered what would make Nick's eyes glaze over like that. What had he been thinking?

The cabin door swung open again. Cool morning air drifted inside, making me shiver. "That was fast. What did—" The words died on my lips.

It wasn't Nick. It was Luke.

Chapter Eight

Luke's tall frame filled the doorway like a dark shadow. His face was no longer a sickly blue but a blazing red, and his eyes held a malicious gleam. A fine layer of snow dusted his black hair and the collar of his leather jacket.

"There you are, you little freak. Have a nice sleepover with your boyfriend?"

"How did you know where I was?" I stood up, a mix of surprise and relief coursing through me.

"John showed me. As soon as we got here, I sent him on his way. It was bad enough I needed him to play tour guide. He doesn't need to know my business." He stepped into the cabin, slamming the door shut behind him. "Why did you bring me in here with you, huh? That wasn't the plan."

"So, you remember what happened?"

His blue eyes glittered. "Not at first. All last night I felt like I was in some kind of goddamn nightmare. Didn't know who I was or how the hell I got here. Then this morning, I was trying to light a cigarette, and my lighter wouldn't work. Worked on that thing for half an hour. And suddenly it all came back to me — how you dumped me in freezing water."

"I didn't *dump* you."

"Were you trying to kill me? Couldn't do it when you were five, but you're a little more powerful now, is that it? Jesus."

"It wasn't my fault," I said through gritted teeth. "You didn't stand back far enough, and the… Never mind. Do you still have the lighter with you?"

"Yeah, in my pocket, like always." He slid his hand in his jacket pocket, as if to reassure himself.

"It acted as your memory trigger."

He narrowed his eyes at me. "You're lucky it didn't fall out when I was in the water."

I blew out a breath. "Just don't let it out of your sight."

"You still have my father's trigger?"

I lifted the dog tags out from under the collar of my shirt. "Got it, but, Luke —"

"Good," he cut in. "Because guess what? I found him."

"What? Where is he?"

"In the café. We stopped in on the way over here. John wanted to make sure you and Loverboy hadn't shown up there this morning. And guess what, Princess? My old man is ready for the loony bin. He thinks he's one of these fucking villagers. He doesn't know me at all, doesn't even know his own name." Luke's eyes bored into mine. "So I need you to come with me. We'll give him his trigger, then you're getting us the hell out of here."

I chewed on my lip. "I don't think it's going to be that simple."

"And why not?"

"Because the trigger I brought for Nick hasn't worked. I gave him the picture, and he's been carrying it around with him...but it didn't trigger his memory."

The hardwood floor creaked under his boots as he crossed the room. Gripping my arm, he said, "Are you telling me he's had that picture since yesterday, and he still thinks he's part of this crazy world, too?"

"Yeah. And I've told him about his life, about the fire, about us." I drew in a shaky breath. "He doesn't remember any of it."

"You better hope it's different for my father."

"That's just it, Luke. I don't think it will be. Your father and Nick have been in here for two months. Like I told you before we got here, the longer someone is in a painting, the longer it takes for them to get their memory back, even with a trigger."

"Yeah, yeah," he said, his voice tinged with impatience. "I know you did. But I was thinking a couple of hours at most."

"Well, I guess the trigger needs more time to sink in or something. But I think if we give them constant reminders about who they really are, it'll help," I added, having no idea if that were true. We had to try something, though. It was only a matter of time before the village was painted over.

"Jesus, Parsons. You think I want to hang around this hellhole and walk down memory lane with my old man?"

"I don't like this any more than you do, but it's our only option. I can't send them home until they're themselves again."

"There must be another way." Luke curled his mouth in disgust, as if the idea of talking to his father about their life in the real world was totally abhorrent, which again begged the question—if life with his dad was so horrible, why was he so desperate to have him back?

"Luke—"

"You already ran off to find your boyfriend after you dropped me in that freezing water." He leaned in, eyes glinting, his breath hot on my face. "Now it's time for you to fix what your mother did. You're going to find a way to get my father's memory back...and fast."

"I'll give him the trigger, but then the rest is up to you."

"I think you're lying." He dug his fingers into my arm. "You have those freaky powers. You've got to be able to do something."

"Let her go," said a loud voice.

Nick stood in the doorway, his fists clenched at his sides, his face steely.

Luke stared at Nick, recognition in his ice blue eyes. "*You*," he said, the single word dripping with disdain. "You screwed things up for me before. You're not going to do it again."

Nick took a step forward, his lips tight. "I said let her go." His voice was cold and calm, but he flicked his eyes to mine, and I saw a spark of rage in their brown depths.

"Why do you care if I touch her?" Luke sneered. "From what I hear, you don't even remember her."

"And from what *I* hear, you're a major pain in the ass. Now, for the last time, let her go."

Luke dropped his hand. "Back off, man. I didn't hurt her."

Nick glared at him. "Just get away from her."

A smirk crossed Luke's face as he took a few steps back. "Well, well, look who's the knight in shining armour."

A muscle twitched in Nick's cheek, and I could tell he was struggling to contain the anger that flowed beneath the surface. It seemed I wasn't the only one who needed to keep strong emotions under wraps. His eyes searched my face. "Are you okay?"

"Yeah," I said, massaging my arm. "I'm telling you the truth, Luke. I don't know of an instant way to get your father's memory back."

Luke looked at me intently for one long moment. "You better *not* be lying."

"I swear, I'm not."

He gave me a brusque nod. "Fine. Let's go give Tom his memory trigger then."

"I have to go with Luke to the café. Will you come?" I asked Nick.

"Damn right I will," he said. "No way am I leaving you alone with him."

My mouth fell open a little, surprised by the intensity of his expression. Luke was right. For someone who claimed not to know me, he was acting awfully protective.

And outside, he insisted on taking me in the sleigh again.

"Really? The princess is too good to walk?"

"Her ribs are bruised," Nick said tersely. "You can shut up and get in or walk. Your choice."

"Fine. Whatever." Letting out a snort of disgust, Luke folded his body in beside me.

For several minutes the only sound was the runners cutting through the snow and the soft whistle of the wind in the trees. Luke's gaze darted between Nick and me, finally coming to rest on the back of Nick's head. "So it must be pretty sweet, having that cottage all to yourself. What's that all about?"

"I don't have any family here, so I live on my own."

"At seventeen?" Luke scoffed.

Nick shrugged. "It's no big deal."

"It'd be a big freakin' deal in the real world, Loverboy. This place is seriously screwed up."

Nick continued to stare straight ahead, but he stiffened. "What did you just call me?"

"You know," Luke said, laughing. "Loverboy. Isn't it an accurate name, after spending the night with Julia?"

"Shut *up*, Luke," I said, "or I'll open a portal and send you out of here."

"You're bluffing."

"Am I? You sure you want to take that chance? If I send you home, you won't have a clue what's going on with your dad in here. Is that what you really want?"

The taunting light faded from Luke's eyes. "No."

"Then I suggest you focus less on us and more on your father. You might've called the shots back home, but in here"—I waved a hand to indicate our painted surroundings—"I hold the cards. Don't forget that."

Luke jaw tightened. "And I know a secret about your magic. Don't forget *that*."

I didn't bother responding to that. I still wasn't sure there *was* a secret.

We pulled up to the café. With a last sour look my way, Luke climbed down from the sleigh and disappeared inside. Nick dismounted and stared after him, not moving.

"Nick? What is it?"

He tore his gaze from the café and focused on me. "What an asshole. You handled him pretty well, though."

"I'm trying not to let him get to me, but it's not easy. He likes to twist things around. And he has a lot of issues. His big one right now is that he's pissed my mother sent his father here."

"He seems to know a lot about my relationship with you."

I snorted. "Yeah, right. He likes to think he knows all sorts of stuff about... Wait a minute. Are you starting to believe what I've told you?"

He heaved a sigh. "Both you and Luke think I'm this Nick guy, so I don't know what to believe."

"You don't remember Luke being in my house when the fire broke out?"

"No. Like I said, I don't remember anything about a fire. But..." He put out his hand to help me out of the sleigh.

I wanted to keep holding onto him, but he let go as soon as my feet touched the ground. "What?" I prompted, trying to ignore the twinge of disappointment. "Did you have a memory of something else then?"

"Not an actual memory. More like a feeling that I *wanted* to remember something, but I couldn't figure out what, exactly. I don't know if that makes any sense."

I knew just what he meant. I'd experienced something similar when I'd been struck by the image of the teddy bear. "It does. When did that happen?"

"In the cabin. When you took my hand."

"Oh." A sensation of warmth flooded my heart. "I think that's a really good sign."

"Then when I came in and saw Luke… Well, it's like he said. I *did* feel protective. Insanely protective."

Now my heart swelled with hope. Was it possible he was starting to feel something for me? Or was his reaction just instinctive? He'd probably want to protect *anyone* from Luke. I shook off the last thought and smiled up at him. He smiled back, a small crooked grin that I'd look at forever if I could.

In the café, the smell of fresh bread and apple pie wafted under my nose. Half of the tables were filled with patrons. They all glanced up with welcoming smiles.

We found Luke standing next to a table near the counter. A short, dark-haired man sat there alone, shovelling pasta and garlic bread into his mouth like it was the first meal he'd eaten in a long time. His forehead puckered in concentration as he chewed.

Luke stared at him in disgust, loudly clearing his throat.

The man looked up. "Oh!" he said, swallowing. "Hello…ah, Lyle, was it?"

"Luke."

"Right, of course. I see you brought your friends." He nodded at Nick. "And you know Daniel? How are you doing, son?"

"Fine, sir," Nick said. "This is Julia."

"Pleased to meet you. I'm Dave." He rose to shake my hand, meeting my eyes briefly before settling back down to his food. "Please, everyone, sit."

Luke dropped into a chair next to his dad, crossing his arms. Nick and I took seats on the other side of the table.

Dave broke off a hunk of bread and shoved it in his mouth. "You should all order some lunch. The food here is delicious."

"We're not here to eat," Luke said. "We need to talk to you about…your situation."

"Oh, that's right," Dave said, raising his scraggly eyebrows. "You think I'm your father. But, as I told you earlier, I don't have a son."

Luke shot me a look as if to say '*I told you so*'.

I stared at Dave-Tom, his cheeks stuffed with noodles, his chin smeared with tomato sauce. This was Luke's father? I didn't remember him from when I was five, and at the moment he was a far cry from the unstable, vengeful man Luke had made him out to be. He had a long, narrow face that was broken up by a contented smile as he ate.

"You don't remember Luke?" I asked. "Are you sure?"

He gave Luke a cursory glance before taking a drink of water. "No, afraid not." He chuckled in wonderment. "I think I'd remember having a son."

I leaned forward slightly, careful not to press my ribs against the edge of the table. "What Luke says is true. You're his father and your name is Tom. You don't live here. You're from a little city called St. Peter's. My mother sent you here."

He waved a hand at Luke. "That's what he said. I don't know what you're talking about. I've always lived here."

"Think back," I said. "You don't have memories of growing up here, right?"

He paused with another forkful halfway to his lips. "No, I don't. But I don't recall anything else, either. This is home."

"This girl here, her full name is Julia Parsons," Luke said. "You saw her mother on the news. Charlotte Parsons."

Tom pursed his lips. "Nope, never heard of either one of them."

"Oh, come on. This is the girl you've held a grudge against for years. She's a freak of nature. You've got to remember what she tried to do to me. You brought it up every time I didn't live up to your expectations."

He frowned. "A freak of nature? Come now, boy. Don't insult the girl."

"Yeah, that's enough, Luke," Nick said sharply.

I lifted Tom's dog tags from around my neck and held them out to him. "What about these? Do you recognise them?"

Tom wiped his hands on a napkin before taking the tags from me. "Hmm. TR Mercer. CDN Forces. What does that mean?"

"That's your name, old man. Thomas Reginald Mercer. And it means you were in the Canadian Armed Forces."

"Canadian Armed Forces," Tom murmured.

"It's the military," I explained. "You served in Afghanistan."

"Afghanistan?" Tom laughed. "What's that?"

Luke's face went red and I jumped in before he could speak. "Will you do something for me, Tom? Ah, I mean Dave? Will you wear the tags? If you put them on and keep them on, this will start to make sense."

"Wear them?" Tom chuckled again. "Are you kids trying to play a trick on me? Why would I wear these? They don't belong to me."

Luke slammed a fist on the table, giving us all a start. "You're living in a fantasy world! If you don't come back to reality, my *friend* here can't get you home. Now put the goddamn tags on!"

A shocked silence fell over the table. I exchanged a look with Nick, then got to my feet. "Luke, can I talk to you alone?"

"Jesus, Parsons—"

"*Now.*"

Luke pushed his chair back from the table with a loud scrape. He muttered something as I led him to the door. Once outside, he grabbed a handful of snow, shaped it into a ball and hurled it at the front of the café. It slammed into the building, then slowly slid down the brick wall before landing in a clump on the ground.

"I know this is hard, Luke. Believe me, I know. I'm going through the same thing with Nick."

He whirled on me, his eyes dark. "It's not the same thing at all. Your boyfriend may not remember who he is yet, but he's bending over backwards for you. He let you stay the night with him, he's defending you—and he gawks at you like he's trying to figure out a puzzle. He's easier to deal with than that crazy bastard in there."

"I told you that it's going to take time. Of course your dad's going to resist what we're telling him. He doesn't know any better right now. But yelling and swearing at him is only going to make things worse. I'll find a way to get him to wear the tags but you need to tone it down. Talk to him, spend time with him. *Help* him remember."

He spat on the ground. "You make it sound easy."

I laughed. "Oh, it's not. It's *so* not. But he's your father, Luke. I thought you wanted to help him."

He turned up the collar of his jacket and shoved his hands in his pockets. "Yeah, yeah. I want to help him. But the old man and me? We don't really talk or spend time together, unless you count his lectures."

That wasn't surprising. I couldn't imagine juvie-bound Luke sitting down for a nice father-son chat. "So, if you can't stand him, why do you want to get him back to St. Peter's so badly?"

"It's none of your business, okay? I'm not in the mood to dissect my relationship with daddy dearest. And you're one to talk. It's not like you and your mother had the perfect relationship. Look at all the secrets she kept from you. And you wanting to be an artist?" he scoffed. "Give me a break. There's no way she supported you, knowing about your ability."

I shrugged. "She never forbade me from painting." With the charm around my neck, I guessed Mom had been confident that other people would be safe from my art. A little *too* confident, as it turned out.

"Maybe she should have." He shook his head. "Why do you do it, anyway? I mean, slapping paint on a wall? I can't think of anything less boring."

I shot him a look. "It's not boring. It's... I don't know, therapeutic. I used to watch reruns of this show called *The Joy of Painting*. It's what first got me interested in art. The host was this guy named Bob Ross. He could make anything with a paintbrush. He painted these really beautiful landscapes, and he had this really cool, kind of hypnotic voice. I remember him saying you can create anything you want with a little imagination. He made me want to create my own worlds."

Luke thumped his hand against the red wall of the café. "Oh, you created a world, all right."

I glanced around at the landscape—buildings that gleamed in the sun, a blanket of the purest white snow I'd ever seen, a sky so dazzlingly bright that it hurt my eyes. Luke wasn't wrong. This was my world, and it would be up to me to open the doorway that led out of it, but first I needed his help.

"We better get back inside," I said. "Just promise me you'll give your dad reminders about who he really is?"

"I guess I don't have much of a choice, do I? That's what you keep telling me, isn't it?"

"Yeah. It is. We have to get their memories back before the mural is painted over." I swallowed. "We're running on borrowed time here."

He kicked at a bank of snow. "Fine. If you can sweet-talk him into wearing the tags, I'll try to help him remember."

"All right. But, ah…maybe you should hang out at a different table or something while I talk to him." The last thing I needed was Luke reaching the end of his fuse again before Tom had the tags on.

"I get it. You don't want me spooking him again. Sure…whatever."

Back in the café, Luke sat at a table near the door while I made my way back to Tom. When I got to his table, I was surprised to find that Nick was gone.

"Daniel was needed in the kitchen," Tom explained. He glanced over at Luke, his eyes slightly narrowed.

With a slight wince, I lowered myself onto the chair. "I'm sorry about Luke. He's… He's just a bit anxious right now."

"He's obviously very troubled."

"Yeah, well, things have been hard for both of us. That's why —" I scanned the tabletop for the dog tags and frowned, not seeing them anywhere.

"Looking for these?" His eyes twinkling, Tom pulled down the collar of his plaid shirt. The dull silver chain of the dog tags hung around his neck. "Daniel convinced me to wear them. For some reason, I can't say no to that boy."

My eyes widened. "What did he say?"

"Oh, just that it would really be helping you out if I wore these. Also, it didn't hurt that he promised me free pie as long as I kept them on." He winked at me. "He knows my weak spot. That's for sure."

"Wow." I sat back, floored. Nick still didn't know who he was. He didn't remember me or what he and I had meant to each other, but underneath it all, he was the same Nick—selfless and kind, willing to help without question. A wave of gratitude swept over me. "That's great. Thank you."

He waved his hand dismissively. "Ah, no big deal. I'm still sure it's all a big joke, wearing someone else's tags, but it won't kill me."

"No, it won't. Listen… I have another favour to ask you."

"Another?" He arched an eyebrow. "And what would that be?"

"Like you said, Luke is troubled. He's new here and honestly—and you didn't hear this from me—he's scared, being in a strange place." I hesitated, hoping Tom would be as helpful as Nick. "I was wondering if you could spend the afternoon with him."

"Hmm." Tom picked up the coffee cup sitting at his elbow and took a drink. "You're new here too, aren't you? Are *you* scared?"

I gave him a tight smile. "I was…at first. But I had Daniel to show me around yesterday. And it really helped. If you could do the same for Luke, I would really appreciate it."

"Well, I like to help out when I can. That's what folks do around here." Tom leaned across the table and lowered his voice. "But your friend Luke seems a bit unstable."

Funny, that was exactly how Luke had described his father not that long ago. "Right," I agreed. "And if you let him tag along with you this afternoon, I think it'll calm him down."

Tom glanced at me before taking another sip of his coffee. Then he set the mug down with a chuckle. "You seem like a nice girl, but you kids are way off course if you think I'm this boy's father. Even so, Luke can come with me to the pub. I have work to do there this afternoon. And it won't be long before I prove to him that I'm not the man he's looking for."

I nodded. "Fair enough." I signalled to Luke, who came over with a scowl darkening his face. "Dave says you can hang out at the pub while he does some work. Isn't that great?"

"Wonderful."

I narrowed my eyes and muttered, "Be nice."

Luke pasted a smile on his face and said, "Thanks, Dave." His gaze fell on the dog tags. "Would you excuse us for a second?"

"Certainly."

Taking me by the elbow, Luke pulled me a few feet away from the table. "How did you get him to wear them so fast?"

"I didn't. When I got back to the table, he was already wearing them."

"What?"

"Nick convinced him." I felt a surge of pride when I said it.

"Huh. Looks like Loverboy might come in handy. And there he is now." Luke jerked his chin in the direction of the kitchen, where Nick had just stepped out. "What do you have planned for him while I'm working on my father?"

"I haven't figured that out yet." He was on the verge of remembering something. I had to believe that. As long as we were together, as long as I had more chances to remind him who he was, I didn't care what we did.

He headed towards me, carrying a large brown paper bag, irritation etched on his face. Stacey followed close at his heels. "Daniel!" Her voice was shrill, her mouth turned down in a pout. "We haven't finished talking."

Nick turned and drew Stacey back towards the kitchen door. He kept his voice low as he spoke to her, so I didn't hear what he said, but her reply was loud and clear.

"How can you do this to me? After everything I've done for you, you run off with some strange girl? How can you betray me like this?"

He shook his head and took a step away from her. She caught his arm.

"She's filling your mind with lies. Can't you see that?"

Now his voice rose. His words were steady and even, but they had a distinctive edge. "I have to see this through. If you care about me at all, you'll let me do that."

"I do care." Stacey twined her fingers in his hair and locked her eyes on his. Disgust curled in my belly. "That's why I'm afraid for you, afraid that she's brainwashing you. That she's trying to take you away from me."

Nick reached up and gently disengaged her hand. "I'll be fine. I'll see you later, okay?"

Leaving Stacey to gape after him, he hurried over to me. "Sorry about that." He gestured to the bag. "I have a couple of deliveries to make. You can come along if you want—or if you're too sore, I can—"

"I'll come," I interrupted. There was no way I was letting him out of my sight. "Luke is going to stay with Dave."

"Great. Let's go." He weaved through the tables, obviously in a hurry to get out of the café. When he held the door open for me, I couldn't help glancing back before I walked out.

Stacey watched me from the kitchen doorway, her green eyes hard and cold. A shiver ran through me even before I crossed the threshold and stepped out into the wintry air.

The body type and facial features were different, but the contemptuous look on her face reminded me of Trisha.

Chapter Nine

"Are you sure you're okay to do this?" Nick asked as the sleigh started moving away from the café.

"I'm sure." I hesitated. "I heard what you said to Stacey, about wanting to see this through. Did you mean it?"

He glanced over his shoulder at me, his expression unreadable. "I did." He shook his head and faced forward again. "This whole other life you've told me about? It sounds so crazy, so unbelievable. But I have this strange feeling. I can't explain it. Like something's not right."

My pulse quickened and hope bloomed in my heart again. Maybe his memory trigger *was* starting to work. "Nothing's right about this situation," I said softly.

"You guys really think Dave is Luke's father? That just blows my mind."

"Yeah." A knot twisted in my stomach as I pictured Luke losing his patience with his father at every turn. If he didn't go easy on him, he would only make things worse. "By the way, thank you for getting him to wear the tags."

"No problem. Dave's a pretty simple guy. He just needed a little persuasion."

"Well, it was a big help. More than you know. I know you don't understand why it's so important— I mean, not *really*."

He shrugged. "It's important to you, and that's good enough for me."

I stared at his broad shoulders, stunned. Before I could respond, though, he pulled up in front of a little cottage. Smoke drifted lazily from the chimney. "This is my first stop."

"Can I come with you?"

"Ah, sure."

At Nick's knock, the door was opened by a petite elderly woman with silver-grey hair that was pulled back in a loose bun. When she saw Nick, her violet-coloured eyes lit up behind her glasses, her cheeks pinking in delight.

"Hello, Daniel! How are you today?"

"Fine, Mrs. Burke. And you?"

"Oh wonderful, now that you're here. And I see you brought a friend. Come in, come in, both of you."

As we stepped into the warm, cheery cottage, I couldn't help staring at Mrs. Burke. I knew every inch of her wrinkled face because I'd taken such care to get it right, to capture the kindly features of the woman who stood in front of the church in my painting. Now she bustled around her cottage, moving aside her knitting so we could sit on the plump, flower-printed loveseat, setting the container of soup Nick brought her on the kitchen counter, and finally, leaning down to give Nick a motherly peck on the cheek.

"Bless your heart, Daniel. You know how Doris' soup warms my feeble little body."

Nick laughed. "You're not that feeble, Mrs. Burke. You've got more energy in your little finger than most people in the village."

"True, true," she said, taking a seat on a rustic rocking chair. She looked at me with a sly smile. "He knows I could easily take a little jaunt over to the café for my daily soup, but I prefer to have him deliver it. I do so enjoy our chats."

"So do I, Mrs. Burke."

She squinted at me a little over her glasses. "You're Deborah's granddaughter, aren't you? Or Kathy's, maybe? You'll have to forgive me. My memory is not as good as it used to be when it comes to names and faces."

"Actually, Julia is —"

"Kathy's granddaughter." I cut Nick off before he could tell Mrs. Burke I was new to the village. It seemed easier this time to pretend I was someone else. *Fewer questions that way.* Thankfully, Nick followed my lead.

"That's right," he said. "She wanted to give me some company today."

"Oh, how nice. I can tell you're a kindred soul, Julia, just by looking at you." She treated me to a wide smile. "Not like that daughter of Doris'. What's her name again, Daniel?"

"Stacey," Nick said with a tight smile.

"Right. One of my neighbours told me she's always hanging over you, causing a scene. You'd be better off with a lovely girl like Julia here."

Nick's face went red with embarrassment. "I'm not *with* Stacey, Mrs. Burke."

"Well, I'm glad to hear that," she said, winking at me. "Now you just wait here a moment. I have your sweater ready for you."

She disappeared into her bedroom and returned with a thick wool sweater. It was fire engine red with a trio of snowman on the front. "Here you go, dear," she said, laying it in Nick's lap. "Only took me a few days to finish."

"It's beautiful." Nick kissed her cheek. "Thank you. I can't wait to wear it."

"The colour will match the scarf I knitted you last week."

"Oh, I never even thought of that. You're right."

I hid a smile as he folded the sweater. "That's really thoughtful of you, Mrs. Burke."

"It's the least I can do," she replied, patting him on the shoulder. "He's wonderful company. Best part of my day."

After chatting with Mrs. Burke for a few more minutes, we said goodbye.

Outside, Nick told me he only had one more delivery to go, and it turned out to be Dr. Evans. When we arrived, he whisked us inside, accepted an apple pie from Nick with a smile, then turned to me. "How are the ribs holding up today? Much pain?"

"Still a bit sore," I said, "but so much better than yesterday."

"Good to hear. Now you keep using the compresses, all right? If you do, the rest of the pain will be gone in no time." He paused. "I trust that Daniel has been taking good care of you?"

"He has, yes."

"I wouldn't have expected any less. Do you know he chopped a half a cord of firewood for me when I ran out? I'd been tending to an injured young man and came back to find it stacked outside my door, waiting for me."

I smiled. "That doesn't surprise me at all."

As we left the doctor's cottage, Nick gave me a sideways glance. "What?" he said with a laugh. "What's that grin for?"

"It's just... You've been trapped in here for two months and you're still the same old Nick. I thought you wouldn't be, but you are. You're still generous and caring and selfless. You take soup to little old ladies and pretend to like the ugly sweaters they knit you. You chop firework for the busy doctor." I stepped into his cottage when he held the door open for me. "And you... You don't even remember me and you take care of me."

He closed the door behind him and took off his hat. A lock of hair fell across his forehead. I ached to touch it, to touch him, but I willed myself to stay where I was in the middle of the room, waiting for his reaction.

"That's nothing," he said with a shrug. "Anyone would do it."

"No, they wouldn't. You help people. That's what you do. It's why you won that humanitarian award. It's why one of your greatest ambitions is to work with Doctors Without Borders someday. You're amazing."

He rubbed his neck. "Wow. High praise. I don't know what to say to that."

"You don't have to say anything. I just wanted you to know that no matter how much you believe you're someone named Daniel and that your life is here, you haven't lost your sense of self. You're still you. I know this all sounds crazy to you, but it's the truth."

"It could be a coincidence, that your Nick and I are a little bit alike."

"No," I said firmly. "It's not."

He was quiet for a moment, still rubbing his neck as he did when he was uncomfortable. His gaze darted around the cottage, as if it was too much for him to look at me. I could practically see the thoughts and questions racing through his head, but he didn't voice any of them.

"I know it's a lot to hear, but you can ask me anything."

He pulled off his jacket, held his hand out for my coat and hung them on the rack by the door. When he turned back, he finally made eye contact with me. "Going through a portal. It sounds pretty dangerous. Both you and Luke got hurt while doing it."

Disappointment snaked around me. I'd hoped he would ask me about his life with me. "I don't think it's always like that," I answered, thinking of my soft, cushiony landing in the poppy field. "But I guess the bigger the portal, the more risk of getting hurt. More places to land in, maybe. My mural is pretty big."

Nick pushed his hands through his hair. "How can we be *in* a painting, Julia? This is a village with real people in it."

"That's the thing, Nick. No matter how much they seem real, they aren't. You and I, and Luke and his dad? We're the only real people here. And we don't belong here. Deep down, I think you know that."

"All I know is that something doesn't feel right to me all of a sudden." He blew out a breath. "All right. So, if you really did get here through a portal, what did you do to open it? You said strong emotions conjure them, so I'm just wondering, what were you feeling to get in here?"

"Anger," I said, "and sadness. Luke was going on about the fire and being an asshole like usual, making me think of all the awful things that happened to me and to you and Mom. As much as I hated him for doing that, I have to admit that it made me get in here pretty quick. But feeling really sad and mad like that is insanely uncomfortable. All my life, it's been so easy for me to push my feelings back. I'm not used to...well, feeling so much."

"Why couldn't you try remembering happy times?" he asked. "Does the emotion always have to be dark?"

"I think so," I said, shrugging. "Those are usually the strongest ones."

"Jeez." He shook his head. "It sounds rough."

I eased myself onto the sofa bed with a wince, feeling achy after the events of the morning. "It's not the kind of ability I ever would've wished for, but I've got it."

"You okay?"

"Yeah. Just a little tired."

"Lie back. I'm going to get another compress for you."

I propped myself against the pillows and gratefully accepted the cider-soaked compress when Nick brought it in. He set a mug on the table beside me.

"I'll be right back. Just going to put Dusty away."

Alone, I held the compress against my ribs. Countless questions flew through my head — things like how was Luke doing with his father and what was Nick thinking? And the biggest question of all...what was I going to do if he didn't regain his memories before the mural was painted over?

Pretty soon I was worn out from all the agonizing. My brain needed a break. *I* needed a break. Settling back on the bed, I closed my eyes and tried to clear my mind.

I was standing in front of the house on Ennis Avenue. It was a calm, clear day. Not a puff of breeze in the air, not a cloud in the sky. But there was a storm raging inside of me, bubbling up in my chest and screaming to be let out. I wanted everyone to go away so I could focus on getting rid of it.

But that boy Lucas was bothering me again, asking me to come play in his yard. And he had that scummy teddy bear with him, as usual.

"Come on, Julia," he said. "I want you to come over."

Didn't he know I felt too awful to play? Why couldn't he understand that I needed to be alone with my feelings?

"Go away," I called, tears flowing down my heated face like a river. "Just go away."

"Why? What's wrong?"

The storm reared up like a violent horse, its hooves beating against my chest. If he wouldn't listen, I'd have to make him go away. There was a Smurfs poster hanging in my room. I wanted him in there, where he would leave me alone. "I told you to go away!"

My scream echoed down the street. I swayed on my feet, dizzy. My eyes closed. When I opened them again, a doorway filled with a bright blue and white light floated next to Lucas. His teddy bear was pulled from his arms and shot through the door like a bullet.

Someone was shaking me.

I woke with a jolt, my face and hair damp with sweat. Nick pulled me into his arms. "Hey, it's okay. I'm here."

Shuddering, I clutched at him. He held me close, running his hands up and down my back. "It's okay," he repeated. "It was just a nightmare. You're fine."

"God, it was horrible." I buried my face in his shoulder. "It— It was the day I opened the portal and Luke almost went through. I remembered what happened. All of it. I created the door because I wanted Luke to leave me alone. But I didn't mean it. It was like…something took control of me. I swear, I didn't mean to do it."

"I know you didn't," he murmured.

When I finally stopped shuddering, he pulled away, holding me at arm's length. "Okay now?"

I nodded, my heart tripping over itself. Waking up to find his arms around me seemed so normal at first, so *natural*. Those arms had been around me hundreds of times before. But now, watching him move away, his eyes averted, the realization hit me again like a ton of bricks. It wasn't natural for *him* anymore.

Hoping my disappointment didn't show on my face, I got to my feet. "I'm going to go wash up a little."

In the bathroom, I splashed cold water on my face, then just stood staring at myself in the mirror. There were shadows under my eyes and a pallid hue to my skin—or maybe it just seemed that way against the backdrop of my bright surroundings. I reached up with one hand to smooth my swirling mass of hair. Even the blonde highlights looked dull in contrast to the lustrous white of the room.

I leaned my hands on the sides of the sink, trying to steady myself before I headed back out. It was torture, being with Nick…but not being with him. For all my talk of being patient, I didn't know how much more of this I could take.

I opened the bathroom door but stayed where I was when I heard voices.

"You know, Loverboy, I've been wondering how last night went. You and the princess here, all alone. What exactly did you guys do?"

"We talked. She rested."

"So, you didn't 'do it' then? Not surprising. That was the rumour going around school, you know — that she was too much of a prude to sleep with you." I narrowed my eyes into slits. One of Trisha's rumours.

"Don't talk about her like that."

"Bet you thought about hooking up with Trisha Ford," Luke sneered. "Now there's a girl who looks like she's good in bed, even if she is a bimbo."

"Shut up, Luke," Nick said in a tightly controlled voice. "Just shut up."

Luke laughed. "Why? This is the most interesting conversation I've had since I got out of juvie. Come on. Don't tell me you didn't daydream about that cheerleader's hot body and wonder if she looked better in the buff than your girlfriend — or don't you remember?"

With heat rising in my cheeks, I strode to the living room. I got there just as Nick grabbed Luke by the collar, his fist clenched as if ready to strike.

Chapter Ten

My pulse quickened when I took in the expression on Nick's face. His eyes burned with anger as they bore into Luke's, and his cheeks flushed a dark red. The hand on Luke's collar tightened, and his clenched fist trembled at his side.

"Stay back, Julia," he said, his voice hard.

"Sounds like good advice to me, Princess." Luke stared back at Nick, an amused glint in his own eyes. "Looks like Loverboy wants to defend your honour."

An uneasy feeling spread through my stomach. Nick *would* hit him, I knew that. It wasn't like he'd been involved in a ton of schoolyard brawls or anything, but he'd been goaded into fights before by arrogant jocks who couldn't keep their mouths shut.

I bit my lip as I looked from one to the other. If Nick wanted a fight, Luke would give him one. He wouldn't hold back, especially if Nick threw the first punch.

"Nick," I said in a warning voice, taking a step towards them.

He barely glanced at me, his eyes still locked on Luke's. "I'm not going to let him say all that crap about you...about us."

Luke laughed. "You didn't even understand what I was saying. Besides, you don't have it in you."

Nick set his mouth in a tight line. "Want to bet?"

"He's just trying to provoke you, Nick! Walk away."

"I don't think so," he said. He caught Luke's collar in both hands now and gave him a rough shake.

All trace of amusement vanished from Luke's face. His eyes turned ice cold. With a grunt, he clamped his hands on Nick's shoulders and shoved him...hard.

Nick staggered backwards and grabbed the arm of a chair to regain his balance. "You bastard."

A malicious smile spread over Luke's face. "Come on then. You want to do this? Let's do it."

Panting, Nick strode toward Luke. I flung myself in front of him and grabbed his arm. "That's enough! I didn't come in here after you so I could watch you get hurt. Just let it go."

Nick raised his eyebrows. "He's threatened you, constantly insults you — and you want to me to *let it go*? I can't do that."

"You can," I insisted. "He's not worth it."

He glanced sharply at Luke. "Julia, I —"

"I know he's a major asshole. Believe me. Hardly a second goes by when I don't want to punch him out. But it wouldn't help get us out of this mess. And if you fight him and get hurt — if both of us are hurt — then we're screwed."

His eyes softened. "All right. I'll let it go...for now."

"Jesus, Parsons. You didn't tell me your boyfriend had such a temper."

"What are you doing here?" I demanded. "Why aren't you with your father?"

Luke pulled out his cigarette lighter and twirled it between his fingers. "I tried, all right? I did what you said. I talked to him about our life in St. Peter's, about his stint in the military and blah, blah, blah. He didn't want to listen to any of it."

I pressed my fingers to my eyes. "You didn't give it enough time."

"Oh, I gave as much as I could stand. It's pointless."

"It's not. You're just not trying hard enough."

"Really?" Luke said with a sneer. "What about what you're doing with Nick here? I don't see *you* making much progress. Does he remember you yet? Does he remember *anything*?"

Before I could answer, Nick touched my sleeve. "Julia."

I turned to look at him. The anger had disappeared from his face, and there was an urgency in his eyes that made the hairs on the back of my neck stand up. "What is it?"

"I do remember something."

I drew in a breath. "You do?"

"Yeah. It came to me all of a sudden when you went to the bathroom. I was going to tell you, but then *he* showed up," he added, jerking his head at Luke.

"Tell me."

"I remember…M&Ms."

Luke rolled his eyes. "Oh, give me a break. Of all the things in the real world for you to remember, it's *candy*?"

I barely heard Luke's snarky comment over the wild beating of my heart. I fastened my eyes on to Nick. "What about them?"

Nick licked his lips, his gaze moving rapidly over my face. "I gave them to a little girl when she fell off her bike and skinned her knees. I wanted her to feel better."

"That's right," I said in a husky voice.

"I saw it in my head. I crossed the street to give her the M&Ms, then my mother came out of my house after me. But the girl... It was you, wasn't it?"

I nodded, tears stinging the back of my throat. "Yes."

"I knew it. This memory? It kind of feels like it belongs to someone else, but I see it so clearly in my mind." He smiled at me. "And when it came to me, somehow I knew you were the girl."

"You're remembering the day we met." I wanted to throw my arms around him and weep in relief. "Do you remember anything else?"

"No. Just that one memory. It seems out of place with everything I know, but I think it really happened."

"It happened. Things are starting to come back to you. You see?" I shot Luke a look of triumph. "His memory trigger *is* starting to work. Now it won't be long before your father's does, too."

"Shit," Luke said, his eyes round with disbelief. "Maybe you're right."

* * * *

I stood in front of the village pub. It occupied a space at the end of a narrow lane, just where I had painted it in my mural. A trio of tall fir trees stood in a row to one side of it. A narrow stream flowed on the other side, a small foot bridge arching over the strip of crystal-clear water. I stopped and stared, amazed at how both the stream and the bridge shone like silver in the moonlight.

I turned my attention to the pub. The long, narrow building had a thatched roof, a coat of gleaming white paint and windows made of frosted glass. Lush green bushes flanked a curving stone walkway. Over the door hung a rectangular sign that read *Village Pub* in curling black script.

"Julia? You okay?"

I turned to look at Nick. "I'm fine. It's just that all of this is too familiar. It makes me feel kinda sick."

He nodded but didn't say anything. He'd been strangely quiet on the way over. I was glad Luke had rushed ahead of us into the pub. Now I had a chance to talk to Nick alone.

"How about you?" I asked. "How are you doing?"

"I…" He glanced at the door of the pub, then back at me with a slight laugh. "I feel strange. Disoriented." He slipped his hand in his pocket and withdrew the picture. It was creased in the middle and curling at the edges. "When you first showed this to me, it didn't make any sense. All I kept thinking was how could I have been at this house, with you, and not remember it. But now…"

"Now?" I prompted.

"Now I think I was there. Somehow I just know that this *is* me."

"It was you." I felt a wistful smile cross my face. "Your parents hosted a party for us that night. And when you walked me home, you—"

"I kissed you for the first time," he finished.

My heart skipped a beat. "Do you remember?"

He pocketed the picture with a rueful laugh. "No. You told me yesterday."

"Oh. Right. Well, I remember it." Before I could stop myself, I put my hand on his face and stroked a line along his jaw. I was filled with an intense longing to feel his lips on mine again. "It was one of the best moments of my life."

He drew in a sharp breath, his eyes trained on mine.

The door of the café burst open and Luke stuck his head out, scowling. "You coming in sometime this century?"

Startled, I dropped my hand. "Yeah, coming," I called.

Nick stepped back, rubbing the back of his neck. "I guess we better go in."

"Right," I said again, my cheeks burning. "Let's go."

He held the door open for me, and when I stepped over the threshold, the noise hit me like a wave. It seemed like every villager was packed inside the pub. They lined up in a scraggly row at the bar, crowded around the fire that roared in the large stone hearth, crammed into booths and squeezed around tables. A few even lounged on upholstered window seats. The flickering candles placed on each table gave the dim pub a cosy glow.

The counter behind the bar was filled with bottles of varying shapes and sizes. They housed an assortment of liquids—rich red, golden amber, clear and shimmering—all winking against an exposed flagstone wall.

The laughter and chatter abated as we entered but returned with a roar as people came forward to greet us. Some pumped my hand, some patted my arm, all welcoming me in, their voices hearty and loud, their faces shining. I endured it with sweaty palms and a churning stomach, wishing for an escape. It was one thing to meet a couple of villagers, but to have an endless throng of them pushing against me was something else entirely.

This isn't real. None of you are real.

Just when I thought I couldn't take it anymore, a voice boomed over the crowd. "All right now, let's give the girl some air."

It was Susan, threading her way through the crowd until she was close enough to take my hand. Before I could say a word, she pulled me towards the bar. I glanced over my shoulder at Nick. He called out to me, but his words got swallowed up in a fresh wave of loud chatter. He disappeared in a sea of people. I didn't see Luke anywhere.

Susan led me to a bar stool and took my arm to help me up onto it. "How are you feeling?" she asked.

"I'm okay. I'm sorry I didn't come back for Luke. When I found N — Daniel — he wanted to take me to his cottage."

She waved a dismissive hand. "Say no more. Doris explained the whole thing to me. I'm just happy you had a quiet place to rest."

I shifted uncomfortably on the bar stool. "Ah, yeah. I guess it probably wasn't too quiet for you when Luke woke up."

"Well, I won't argue with you there," she said, laughing. "That boy was fit to be tied."

"And didn't that bother you?"

"No, dear. Not really." Her laughter died down, but she kept smiling that eerily bright smile of hers. "He was understandably upset that you'd left. That's all."

"Still, I'm sorry you had to deal with him. I know what he's like."

"Don't trouble yourself about it, Julia. I only spoke with him for a moment before he went off in search of you. Besides," she added, treating me to a glimpse of her startlingly white teeth, "not much bothers me. I'm just glad he found you. I saw you come in together."

"You're just happy about everything, aren't you?" I muttered.

"What was that, dear?"

"Nothing. Ah, listen… Have you seen Dave? I need to talk to him."

"Right here," said a voice at my side.

I turned to find Luke's father staring at me, his expression inscrutable. "Come with me."

"Where?"

He bent close to me so he could be heard over the escalating noise. I could smell alcohol on his breath. "Just outside for a minute, where it's quiet. I want to talk to you."

"I really should find Daniel first," I shouted.

"We'll find him after."

He took my arm and guided me through the crowd in much the same way Susan had done. We squeezed our way through the press of bodies towards the door. The urge to escape the overheated room grew stronger by the second.

After what seemed like ages, we made it to the door. Outside, the evening breeze was like a cool caress on my burning face. I stood with my back against the wall of the pub, breathing in the pine-scented air.

"It even smells lifelike," I said.

"What?" Dave raised his eyebrows.

"Never mind." I waved a hand. "So, what did you want to talk to me about? Is anything coming back to you?"

He laughed, shaking his head. "Well, that's just it. I let that Luke boy hang around with me this afternoon. It was the neighbourly thing to do. But then I had to listen to him go on and on about how I'm his father and his mother left us." He fingered the dog tags. "I even let Daniel talk me into wearing these things. Now it's time for you to tell me what you kids are up to."

"We're not up to anything. Everything Luke told you is the truth. And if you—"

"Are you bored? Got nothing better to do than try to get a rise out of me? Is that it?"

"No." I pushed my hands into the pockets of the coat I'd borrowed from Susan. "That's not it at all."

His thin lips stretched in a condescending smile. It was a far cry from the warm, friendly smile he'd worn earlier. *Is Tom's personality starting to show through? Did Luke trigger something in him, after all?*

"I get it," he said. "You're new here, so you may not understand how things are in this little village."

"Oh?" I arched a brow. "And how is that?"

He shuffled closer. His eyes sharpened and latched onto my face in a way that made a shiver glide down my spine. "We don't play tricks on each other. The young people that live here? They respect their elders. So why don't you and your friend stop this charade and go back to wherever you came from."

"But you don't understand."

"Oh, I understand plenty. I understand you've gotten your kicks out of wasting my time. Now let's go find Luke so you can be on your way." This time when he took my arm, his grip was anything but gentle, his fingers curling around my biceps painfully. I clenched my teeth, about to pull away, but before I could, he dropped my arm like it was on fire.

"What the hell?" He took a hasty step backwards, horror written all over his narrow face. "There's something wrong with you."

A shudder ran through me. "What? What are you talking about?"

"You're trying to mess with my mind somehow, aren't you?"

"No, I—"

"I saw you. Just now, in my head. You were a little girl, and you did something horrible. I just don't remember what it was." He put his hands on his temples as if he were in pain. Then he lifted his eyes to meet mine again. They were cold and hard like his son's. "What did you do?"

I looked down at my boots. "When Luke and I were kids, I almost sent him away. You were angry. But you have to understand that it was an accident."

"I didn't know you when you were a kid, so how am I seeing you in my mind?"

"It's a memory. Your dog tags... They're starting to trigger memories of your life in St. Peter's." I paused, trying to choose my words carefully before I spoke again. Tom needed to remember that life before he could go back through a portal, but I was pretty sure he wasn't going to like the parts that included me.

I was saved from having to continue, though, because at that moment Nick burst out of the pub. His gaze flicked between us a few times before coming to rest on me. "Julia," he said, breathless.

"What is it? What's wrong?"

"I need to talk to you. Alone."

Dave backed up to the door, shaking his head as if to clear it. "And I need a drink."

"Dave," I said, "if anything else comes to you—anything at all—come find me."

"Right." He staggered a little as he turned to go inside. With one last uneasy look in my direction, he fumbled open the door and disappeared inside the pub.

"What was that all about?" Nick asked.

"He had an image of me as a little girl, just like you did."

"Oh. Well, that's good, right?"

"Yeah. Yeah, it is." But a wave of apprehension washed over me as I recalled the horror in Dave's eyes.

"Julia." Nick crossed the distance between us in three long strides. Taking my hands in his, he let his eyes wander over my face. They gleamed with a kind of certainty I hadn't seen since finding him. "After we went inside, it came back to me."

"What did?"

"Our junior high graduation. I remember it now. Every detail." He released one of my hands. With a touch as light as a feather, he tucked a lock of hair behind my ear, grazing my cheek. My breath hitched. He opened his mouth to continue, but the words caught in his throat. He cleared it and tried again, his voice husky and low.

"You were gorgeous, wearing that white dress. All through the ceremony, you kept looking over at me and smiling. And all I could think about was how much I wanted us to be more than just neighbours, more than just friends. I had it all planned, you know."

"Had what planned?"

He traced the outline of my lips with a fingertip. "I planned to kiss you at the end of the night. And when I did, I remember thinking I was the luckiest guy in school."

"Nick," I breathed. He knew me. He knew *us*...or at least part of what we'd had together.

"I remember you on your bike. And I remember the night I first kissed you. Both of those times are so clear to me now. But everything else is hazy. I just wish that..." He made a deep sound, a cross between a sob and a sigh. "I just wish I could remember the rest. Will you help me?"

"Of course I will, whatever it takes."

His eyes locked onto mine. "I'm not Daniel."

"No," I said, my pulse jumping, "you're not."

"I want to know what it feels like again...to kiss you."

He bent his head and put his mouth on mine. It was the briefest of kisses, just a quick press of his lips, but it sent a million tiny sensations dancing along my spine. When he pulled back, his eyes shone with an intensity that took my breath away. Then he slid his arms around my waist. I desperately wanted him to kiss me again, and I leaned into him, that sense of yearning overpowering any last shred of reason I might have held. This time when he lowered his head, I met him halfway.

At first his lips were soft and tentative, but as soon as I kissed him back, they became more urgent. He pulled me tighter against him, taking the kiss deeper. All thoughts of Luke and Tom and the other villagers fell away. The stress and frustration of being stuck in the mural, of finding a Nick who didn't know himself, poured out of me like water from a fountain. In that moment, no one and nothing else mattered, just me and him and the feel of his body pressed against mine. I was aware of the familiar taste of his mouth and a sensation of blood pounding in my ears. We fit together again, like we had before.

I wanted to sink into him, let myself fall further and further. He tilted his head to change the angle of the kiss, exploring in a way that made my head spin and my body tingle in response. Despite the cold evening, my skin felt like it was on fire.

"What is *this*?"

We broke apart, breathless, and turned to face Stacey, who'd twisted her face in an ugly grimace.

"Stacey —" Nick began.

"What is wrong with you?" she interrupted in a shrill voice. "Why are you kissing her like that? Why are you kissing her at all?"

Nick took a step forward, a patch of red climbing up his neck. "You have to understand. We have a connection."

"No, you don't."

"It's true. I don't think I belong here."

"Of course you do! You can't listen to her, Daniel." Stacey glared at me. "She's just —" She stopped as something on the ground caught her attention.

I followed her gaze.

And my already-thundering heart went into overdrive.

The photograph had fallen from Nick's pocket and fluttered to the ground. It lay on the snow a few feet away, where the evening breeze had likely taken it. I hurried forward. Stacey got there half a second before me and scooped it up.

"Give that to me!" I lunged at her.

She stepped back, holding it out of my reach. "I don't think so. Now what could be so important that —

" The words died on her lips as she took in the smiling faces of me, Mom and Nick. "When was this?"

"Two years ago," I said.

"Where?"

"St. Peter's. It's where I'm from. It's where Nick…well, Daniel is from."

"No, I don't believe it." She continued to stare at the picture, unmoving.

"Will you please give it to me?" My voice was patient, but inside I was screaming at her. Every second that passed by without Nick having the photo in his possession was a second closer to him losing the memories he'd regained.

Stacey lifted her chin. Her eyes narrowed. "No. I won't give it back. Because this is a lie or some kind of trick. And I don't want Daniel looking at this. *Ever again*."

With that, she flung open the door of the pub and ran inside. I followed her, Nick close at my heels.

Back in the suffocating warmth of the pub, I searched for Stacey among the tightly packed villagers. She couldn't have gone too far.

Nick grabbed my arm and pointed. "She's over there."

She was slipping through a knot of people at the back of the pub, the photo still clutched in her hand. Together, we fought our way through the crowd and had almost caught up to her when she stopped in front of the stone hearth.

"Stacey!" Nick said in a sharp voice.

She looked back at us. Her eyes flashed in the light from the fire. Shadows played across her face, giving her a sinister appearance. I watched in horror as she held the picture over the hearth, mere inches from the red-hot flames.

"No!" I stumbled forward. "Don't!"

Before I could reach her, she gave me a cold smile, refocused her attention on the hearth — and dropped Nick's memory trigger into the fire.

Chapter Eleven

Stacey slipped into the crowd. For a split second, I considered going after her, but my feet were planted on the spot and I couldn't stop staring, dumbstruck, as the flames licked furiously along the edges of the photograph. Within seconds, they had eaten away at the paper until there was nothing left but a little pile of black ash settling on the fire logs. The noisy hum of the pub faded into the background as I stayed fixated on the charred remains of Nick's link to the real world. My chest tightened, and I couldn't seem to draw any breath through my lungs. The heat of the flames and the overall warmth of the room came together to make a hot, thick wall around me, squeezing me in. I felt like I was back in my nightmare about the fire on Ennis Avenue.

Don't lose it, I commanded myself. *Stay grounded.*

But even after I counted to ten three times, my throat swelled with emotion. I could feel the frustration and panic mounting inside me. Nick had only just begun to get his memories back. Without the picture, how would he fully find himself again? How would I ever get him back to St. Peter's? There wasn't time to go back home, find another memory trigger and bring it to him. The mural would be painted over any time now. I swiped a trembling hand over my forehead, where beads of sweat gathered across my skin.

"Julia." Nick touched my sleeve. "Are you all right?"

The concern in his voice was almost enough to bring a sob to my lips. "No. That picture… We needed that picture."

"I'm sorry. I don't know what got into her. That was a cruel thing to do." His mouth tightened in a grim line. "I'm going to go after her."

I grabbed his arm. "No, the damage is already done. I just want to get out of here. I-I need a quiet place to think."

He opened his mouth to say something, but he must have seen the panic reflected on my face because he nodded, and without a word, took my elbow to guide me back outside. His touch centred me, and by the time we were in the sleigh, the night air cooling my flushed face, I had gained control of my emotions. It was a tenuous control at best, but it was enough to get me through the ride back to the cottage.

When we arrived, Nick told me to sit down while he made me some tea. But I couldn't sit. I paced the living room, afraid that if I stayed still for even a second, my panicked thoughts would overwhelm me and the line that was currently balancing my emotions would snap.

Nick frowned at me when he emerged from the kitchen, holding a mug. "You're shivering. Get in bed."

"I can't just lie there," I protested. "I have to *do* something. I have to figure this out."

"You can figure it out from there."

Sighing, I slid underneath the covers and reached out to take the mug when he offered it. "You don't understand, Nick. That picture was bringing your memories back. Without it, I don't know what to do. You'll forget again." I bit my lip, dangerously close to tears.

He tucked the quilts around my shaking body, then turned to build a fire. My heart beat furiously in my chest. Why wasn't he saying anything? *Oh God. Is he forgetting already?*

I ran my eyes over the long lean lines of his body as he arranged wood in the fireplace. He threw a match in and when the logs caught, he nudged them with the poker, his movements slow and measured. I swallowed, my mouth suddenly as dry as sawdust.

Turning, he brushed his hands on his jeans. His eyes were distant.

"Nick? Did you lose the memories already?"

He just shook his head and crossed the cabin. He stopped at the front window, his back to me again. The silence wore on as he stood staring out at the dark night, his fingers curled around the windowsill. Finally, I opened my mouth to speak again, but at the same moment he swivelled and faced me. With a jolt of surprise, I realized there was pain in his eyes. "I haven't forgotten."

"Then what is it?"

"I remembered you on your bike and I remembered the night of our first kiss — and I still remember. But not because of a picture." He stepped to the bed and sat down, resting his hand on the quilt. Another inch or so and his fingers would brush against mine. "I think I remember those things because you touched me."

"What?" I said, my voice barely a whisper.

He lifted his mouth in a lopsided smile. "Whenever you've touched me, like for more than a few seconds, it was like something happened to me. I felt this…connection. And every time, I had a flashback. When I held you after your dream, I remembered the day we met. A few minutes after you touched my face outside the pub, the night of the graduation came back to me. I don't think the picture was making me remember." He trained his gaze on my face, the golden flecks in his eyes shining in the firelight. "It was you."

I thought back to those moments when I'd touched him, those moments when it'd been a lingering touch, and realized it was true. Each time he'd been struck by a memory not long after. It *could* have been a coincidence. He'd still had the picture in his possession then. But something else occurred to me. I recalled how Dave had reacted outside the pub when he'd grabbed me. When he'd held on to my arm, he'd had a flashback from the day I'd opened a portal and Luke's teddy bear had been sucked into it. The memory may have been hazy, but it was there.

Maybe it was true then. Maybe touch *could* act as a memory trigger. Hope surged through me. If that were the case, it wouldn't matter that the picture had been destroyed. I could use my touch to bring the rest of his memories back and I could get him home.

I raised my eyes to his. "Wait a minute. I kissed you. What happened when I kissed you? Did you remember something then?"

He nodded. "I came over to your house one day. I don't know when it was, but I think I was carrying a skateboard."

"That would've been about two years ago," I said with a small smile. "You went through a short-lived skateboarding phase around the time we started dating."

"Oh. Okay. Anyway, I let myself in. I heard voices coming from the rec room downstairs. So I went to check it out, to say hello. When I got to the top of the stairs, I realized it was your mom and your aunt. Your mom was saying something like, *'Those two are closer than ever. Thank God for the charm.'* And your aunt said, *'But don't you think she's old enough to know about the magic now?'*"

I felt all the blood drain from my face. "What was Mom's answer to that?"

"I think she said, *'There's no need to tell her. She can live a happy life without ever knowing the magic exists.'* And a second later she came up the stairs, looking a little flustered, but when she saw me, she got totally calm. She just smiled and told me they'd been going over lines for her new play." He shrugged, but he was white-faced. "I believed her."

"You had no reason *not* to," I pointed out.

"No, I should've been more suspicious about the whole thing. Your mom would never have been working on a play about magic. She only ever wrote dramatic scripts." He scrubbed his hands over his stubbled cheeks and let out a ragged breath. "If I'd questioned it, I might've been able to find something out for you."

I laughed. "Mom could lie her way out of a box. She wouldn't have given up the family secret that easily. I mean, look how long she kept it from me."

"But if you had known, you could've been prepared."

I traced a red square of quilt with my finger. "Yeah. I know Mom had her reasons, but leaving me in the dark was a pretty crappy thing to do."

"Exactly. So, if I could've warned you or something…"

"No." I shook my head. "You can't blame yourself. Come on. You overheard a conversation about magic. How could you have known Mom and Aunt Karen were talking about *real* magic?"

"I guess," he said, sighing.

"Never mind that now. I want you to have a better memory. Let's test your theory."

He turned his mouth up in a suggestive smile. "What do you have in mind?"

I took his hand and laced my fingers through his. "This." I looked at him intently, waiting for some sign of recognition to cross his face. He glanced down at our joined hands, stroking his thumb over mine. The gentle caress had me tingling from head to toe. I tightened my hold on his hand, and after a moment, his head snapped up.

"What?" I prompted. "What came back to you?"

"A science fair project. We made papier-mâché models of the planets. We used luminescent paints so they would glow in the dark." He paused, laughing. "And when you tried hanging Jupiter from your basement ceiling, it brought down three tiles."

A wide smile spread across my face. It was working. "That's right. We were in grade eight. You let me play Britney Spears' music the entire time we worked on that project, even though you can't stand her."

"Did we get first place in the fair?"

"Tenth. You kept saying the judging was rigged. You thought we should've won."

"Huh," he said thoughtfully.

"I agreed with the judges actually. There were a lot of projects that were better than ours. But I loved you for saying it." My gaze locked on him again. There was an unexpected tenderness in his eyes. Emboldened, I touched my lips to his, kissing him lightly before I pulled back.

"How about now?"

He made a low sound in the back of his throat. Then, a small nostalgic smile. "Valentine's Day. I told you I loved you and that I'd wait until you were ready."

"Yeah," I said, feeling like my chest was going to burst. "That's right." I let go of his hands so I could push my hair back from my face and gather it into a loose knot at the nape of my neck. All the cold had seeped from my body now and a flush warmed my skin.

He caught my arm. "Don't let go. The memories are coming faster now." His gaze travelled to my mouth. "I want to remember more."

I swallowed. "Okay."

He smoothed his hands over my shoulders and kissed me. His mouth was hungry and insistent this time. I parted my lips and felt the soft tip of his tongue trace mine. He wrapped his arms around me. I melted into him, letting out a quiet moan.

Then the kiss changed. There was a tenderness in the warmth of his lips, in the way his hands caressed my back. It felt familiar.

It felt like home.

After a long moment, he pulled back and held me at arm's length. He searched my face, his caramel-brown eyes clear and focused on mine. He smiled that crooked smile I knew so well and lifted a hand to touch my cheek. "Julia."

My stomach did a backflip. I stared back at him, hardly daring to hope. "What do you remember now?"

When he answered, his voice was soft with wonder. "Everything."

I threw my arms around his neck and pressed my cheek into his solid chest. I could hear his heart, matching the furious beat of my own. A heady mix of relief and joy coursed through me, knocking off the weight that had been sitting on my shoulders. "Thank God." I lifted my head to look at him, to weave my hands through his hair and touch his face as if he might disappear. "Is it really you? You know who you are?"

His arms tightened around me again. "It's me," he whispered into my hair. "God, I feel like I've been dreaming and I just woke up. How could I have forgotten, Julia?"

"It's the mural. It takes away your identity. Makes you believe you're someone else."

"I can't believe you can create portals. If I hadn't seen it with my own eyes, I *wouldn't* believe it."

"I know," I said softly. "I can barely still believe it myself. Bet you never thought your girlfriend would turn out to be a freak."

The knot in my hair came loose and a mass of waves tumbled around my shoulders. Nick tucked a length of it behind my ear. I shivered as his fingers brushed my skin. "Hey, this thing you can do… Yeah, it's pretty crazy. But it doesn't change the way I feel about you, okay?"

"Okay," I said, sighing.

We held each other for another long moment, not saying a word. Then Nick broke the silence. "I'm sorry, Jules."

His voice was filled was raw emotion. I released him so I could look into his face. Tears shimmered in his eyes. "What is it?" I asked. "It's okay. Everything's going to be all right now."

Anguish was carved into his features. "Your mom. I can't believe she's gone. I wish I could've done something. Anything. I'm so, so sorry."

I held up a hand. "No. No pity party now. I thought I lost you both, so from where I sit, I'm grateful. Mom's gone, and that's a nightmare I have to live with every day, but you're here." I smiled. "I'm pretty friggin' happy to have you back. And I'm going to get you home."

He dragged his hands through his own hair now. "I remember everything else, but the fire is all still kind of a blur."

"Well, you were unconscious then you were sucked into the painting. It was a lot to go through." Determined to steer the conversation away from my mother, I said, "What happened when you first got here? Do you remember anything about that?"

"I woke up in the snow in front of the café. At first, I think I knew I'd been sent somewhere, and I tried to hold on to the thought of you. But then Stacey found me, and Doris took me under her wing, and suddenly, I had this new life. Everyone was calling me Daniel and I believed that my life was here. *They* all believed I'd always lived here."

"I wish I'd known you were alive," I said, a tremor in my voice. "I wish I'd known you were trapped here.

I could've come after you sooner. Or if I'd gotten home earlier—"

"If you'd gotten home earlier, you might have been trapped in the fire, too. If you died, who would have saved me, huh?" His eyes twinkled a little.

"Nick…"

He gripped my hand and brushed his lips across my knuckles. "You know it's true," he said. "I mean, against all odds, you followed me here. You came in with some guy who just got out of juvie, and hurting like hell, you found me. Right?"

"Right."

"Because of you, I remember. And I never want to forget again."

His lips recaptured mine. And, feeling the warmth of his mouth and his hands in my hair, any last traces of my guilt and regret subsided. When he pulled back, his face was serious. "I've never wanted anyone but you."

"Ditto." I tilted my head, intending to give him a quick kiss in return, but found my lips lingering on his. He moved his hands up and down my arms, caressing. I sighed as he nuzzled my throat. Swept away on a current of passion, all thoughts of getting us back home flew out of the window.

He trailed kisses down my throat, then sought my mouth again. My body tingled in response. Our legs tangled together. I crushed myself against him, wanting to be as close as possible. He ran his hands under my shirt, stroking my skin. Then he broke away with an unmistakeable question in his eyes.

"Julia?"

"Yes," I said breathlessly. "Yes." To demonstrate that I was ready this time, I pulled the shirt over my head and reached over to help him with his. A moment later, his bare flesh was pressed against mine. Our kisses grew even more heated. I revelled in the feel of him, of solid muscle and curves.

And digging my fingers into his shoulders, I clung to him like I was never going to let go.

* * * *

The best sleep I'd had in two months was interrupted by a pounding on the cottage door. I pried my eyes open and squinted against the blinding rays of morning sun that streamed through the window.

Nick bolted upright beside me. We both scrambled to find our clothes and dressed in record time. I'd just pulled on my shirt when the door flung open. A burst of cold air entered the cabin, and Luke along with it.

"Well, well, well," Luke said with his characteristic sneer, "look who ran away again." He slammed the door and stepped into the living area. He glanced at the rumpled bed, then at my dishevelled appearance. "So, you finally did it? Does this mean you remember who you are, Loverboy?"

"Yeah," he said through gritted teeth. "And I told you to stop calling me that."

Luke laughed. "No way. It fits you more than ever now. Doesn't it, Princess?" His eyes glittered as they ran up and down my body. "Was it everything you imagined it would be? Or did he disappoint you?"

Nick came to stand next to me, putting a protective arm around my shoulders. "What do you think you're doing? You can't just barge in here like this!"

"I can if there's no lock on the door. And seeing that Julia is my ticket out of here, I have a right to know what's going on." His gaze settled on my face. "When were you planning on telling me he got his memory back? In case you forgot, we're up against the clock here."

Crap. He was right. I'd let myself get caught up in the moment with Nick, but we didn't have much time.

"It sort of happened all of a sudden. I — ah, we found out that a person can act as a memory trigger much faster than a personal item. Through touch." I cleared my throat, annoyed that my cheeks felt like they were on fire.

Luke's eyebrows shot up. "You've got to be kidding me."

"You wanted a faster way to get your father to remember, right? I said I didn't know of one, but I was wrong. This is the way, Luke. Touch your father's arm, hug him, hold his hand…whatever. His memory will come back."

"Christ." He scowled as he pulled his lighter and a cigarette from his coat pocket. "Anything else you want me to do? Braid his hair and sing *Kumbaya*?"

"If that's what it takes," I said, my lips twitching. "You're his best chance." *Maybe not his only chance*, I thought, my smile fizzling out. I'd figured that out when Tom held my arm. But it would be better if his memories were triggered by Luke.

"All right. Fine," Luke muttered, putting the cigarette between his lips. "There's just one problem."

Nick frowned. "Don't smoke that in here."

Luke glared at him but pocketed the cigarette and lighter. "Whatever. Cigarettes taste like shit since they got wet, anyway."

"What's the problem, Luke?" I asked.

"I spent all night in the pub with my old man, waiting for him to remember. But he kept knocking back the booze and passed out. By the time he woke up, I was asleep. Next thing I know, Susan is shaking me, telling me I have to go because she's closing up the place. Know what else she told me? That drunken idiot went for a horse ride up into the mountains."

I raised my eyebrows. "After drinking all night?"

"What can I say? He's crazy. Anyway, I'm not going after him by myself."

"I'll come with you." I turned to Nick. "You don't have to stay here anymore. I'll open a portal so you can get back home."

"No way. I'm not leaving you here with him." He watched Luke over my shoulder, his expression stony. "Besides, you guys don't know those mountains. You'll need a guide. It'll be much faster if I go with you."

I hesitated. "I can't risk that you'll forget who you are." I'd just gotten him back, and the thought of losing him again so soon made my chest ache.

He cupped my chin in his hand, his eyes steady on mine. "I won't," he assured me. "Not as long as I'm with you."

"All right." I nodded. "Then let's go. We don't have much time left."

As we piled out the door, I glanced up at the rolling hills. What had once been a backdrop of beauty and serenity in a painting was now a vast and imposing obstacle that made my eyes water. But if I was going to navigate it, I had to stay calm.

* * * *

We climbed up into the hills, me and Nick together on Dusty, while Luke rode the doctor's horse, a gleaming chestnut named Gracie. The horses were quick, making good time through the deep snow. Within minutes we'd left the village behind. We rode through landscape dotted by fir trees and swelling with ice-crusted mounds that winked in the sun.

We called out for Luke's dad until our throats were raw, but the only answer was the wind whistling through the trees. I wrapped my arms around Nick's waist as he guided Dusty along a well-beaten path. My head swivelled as I tried to take in everything, hoping I would catch a glimpse of Tom's dark hair or another horse. But all I could see was the sun bursting through the trees and the layer of dazzling white that covered every inch of our gradual incline. I wrinkled my nose, wishing I hadn't made the snow so clean and pure. In the 3D world of my painting, it was giving me a headache.

Bob Ross had encouraged artists to immerse themselves in their paintings, but this was taking it to a whole new level.

At the first ridge, I glanced behind me, sweeping my eyes over the ground we'd already covered. For just a split second, I thought I saw a flash of movement in a patch of firs, and I asked Nick to stop the horse. But when we backtracked, there was no sign of anyone, just the slow sway of branches in the wind. *Maybe my mind is playing tricks on me.*

When we reached the second ridge, Luke let out a string of curses. "Where the hell is he?"

"He usually doesn't go much farther than this," Nick said. "But maybe he decided to keep going today."

"For frig sakes," Luke muttered. "Help me get off this damn horse, would you?"

"Why?" I asked.

"I need to take a leak, all right?"

"Fine. I guess I could use a quick break, too." I shifted uncomfortably on Dusty, my butt aching. "But we can't stop for long."

Nick slid off Dusty and helped me down before turning to give Luke a hand. As Luke disappeared into a grove of firs, I paced through the sparkling snow, my boots making loud crunching noises. Trees formed a wide semi-circle behind me and the land spread out on either side in undulating patterns that seemed to go on forever. I turned back to stare down the sloping tundra, tugging a hand through my damp, snarled hair as a feeling of cold desperation curled itself around me.

"It's going to be all right," Nick said softly.

"We *have* to find him, Nick. It doesn't matter that he had some kind of vendetta against me. It was my mother who sent him here, *my* family's cursed magic that's responsible for this whole mess."

He caught my hand. "Julia, look at me."

I raised my eyes to his and was surprised by the intense expression on his face.

"You can't blame yourself for this, and you can't blame your mother. No one meant for this to happen."

"Maybe not, but I have to fix it now." I chewed on my lip. "And we're running out of time. The mural is going to be painted over any time now."

He skimmed his eyes over the rolling hills above me, then squinted up at the sun, bright as a flame in the crisp blue sky. "Well, everything looks the same as it always does. I think we're okay for a little longer."

"I hope you're right."

"Hey, we're going to get through this. *You're* going to get through this. You're the strongest person I know."

"I'm not as strong as I used to be." I took a deep breath. "Do you know why Luke calls me 'Princess'?"

He shook his head.

"Because Trisha gave me the nickname 'Ice Princess' after she heard I didn't cry at the memorial service for you and Mom."

"You can't pay any attention to that bitch, Julia. Besides, I understand why you didn't cry. You explained all that to me."

"But she was right," I continued. "I *was* like an Ice Princess. I didn't grieve like most people do because I was cool and calm, in control of my emotions, like usual. The thing is, I'm not like that now. Any little thing can set me off. I'm a freakin' mess, Nick. I've changed. I'm not the same girl you—"

"What?" he cut in, his browns drawn together. "Not the same girl I fell in love with? Don't you dare say that. I told you that my feelings for you haven't changed because you've learned you're a Vista. And what? You think I'm going to run away because you have to work to curb your emotions now, like the rest of us? That only makes you human, Jules. You're still you."

I loved him for saying it, but I didn't want to be this way forever. I didn't know if Luke really did know a secret about getting rid of the Vista magic, but if he did, I was going to get it out of him.

Nick put his arms around me. I rested my head on his shoulder, already feeling steadier in his embrace. Neither of us said anything for a long moment, and as he stroked a hand over my hair, some of the anxious knots in my stomach unfurled.

"Thank God you're here," I whispered.

He laughed. "Told ya you'd want me along for the ride." He tightened his hold on me. "We're in this together, okay? And we *will* find Tom. He can't be too far."

"Jesus," Luke said behind us. "Will you two sappy idiots get a room? Oh, wait. You already did that."

Nick and I broke apart. We both glared at Luke.

"What?" Luke gave us a nasty grin. "I'm only speaking the truth here."

"Yeah well, what you can do is shut up. Don't forget, Julia can—" Nick stopped, frowning at Dusty, whose ears had suddenly perked up. "What is it, boy? What do you hear?"

"I don't hear anything," Luke complained.

Nick shot him another look. "Horses can hear a lot better than humans. There must be something out there."

All three of us trained our eyes along the path, but there was no movement. I was about to suggest we get back on the horses and continue our search when Dusty's ears shot up again, and he tossed his head a little. A few seconds later, another horse came around the bend carrying Tom. He widened his eyes as he approached us. "What the hell is going on here?"

"We've been looking for you, old man."

"Haven't you caused enough trouble, boy?" Tom said, swinging down from the saddle. "You've already played your little games with me, and now you come up here to disrupt my peace and quiet? And I see you've dragged one of our locals with you."

Luke strode over to his father. "Give it up. Nick isn't a local and neither are you."

"Well, you'd like me to think so, wouldn't you?" Tom glanced at me. "You and your friend put some crazy ideas in my head. I had dreams all night about watching some woman named Charlotte on TV then going to her house to find her. Had to come up here to clear my head."

Luke spat on the snow. I cringed. *So much for my unblemished landscape.* "Got news for you. Those weren't dreams. They're memories. They really happened. Charlotte is Julia's mother. You went after her on your stupid, pathetic quest for revenge or to try to fix me or whatever. And because you did that, you ruined all my plans."

"Plans? What's he talking about?" Nick murmured to me.

I shrugged. "No clue."

Tom's face darkened, and he seized Luke by the shoulders. "You're a liar. I don't know you. I don't know any of you."

Luke flicked his gaze to me. I nodded, hoping he understood this was a prime opportunity to use touch to elicit more memories. Obviously, the dog tags had started to work, but we needed to hurry the process along. To my relief, he nodded back, almost imperceptibly. Then he brought his hands up to cover his father's, curling his fingers over them.

"Like it or not, I *am* your son. I've been living under your roof since Mom left."

Tom opened his mouth to toss back another retort, but then he closed it. The anger in his eyes fizzled. A glazed expression passed over his face. "What did you say?"

Luke tightened his grip on Tom's hands. "I already told you all this. Mom left us when I was three. It's been just you and me ever since. We moved to Ennis —"

"Avenue," Tom finished, looking as pale as the snow. He shook off Luke's hands and backed up. "How did I know that?"

"Because you lived there, old man."

Tom licked his lips. "I remember a little girl. She tried to send you away. Did that really happen?"

"Yeah, it happened. And when you went to see Charlotte, she opened a portal and you got sucked in."

"I don't understand."

Luke stepped forward and grabbed his father's wrist. "She was a witch, just like her daughter over there."

A strong wind kicked up snow around us like a sandstorm. I shut my eyes against it. When I finally felt the flurry begin to settle, I opened my eyes and blinked in surprise. The grove, which only a second ago had been bright with morning sun, was suddenly filled with the muted light and lengthy shadows that usually accompanied twilight.

I turned back to Tom. He continued to stare down at Luke's face, immobile. He seemed not to have noticed the abrupt change in light at all. "Charlotte and Julia Parsons," he said in a dazed voice.

"That's right," Luke said. "Do you remember now?"

Tom pulled away from Luke with a gasp, and I could tell from the sudden light in his eyes that the rest of the pieces had fallen into place. "Yes, I do. I went to see Charlotte to get some answers, and she sent me here. She opened some kind of hole and I went through it." He pivoted towards me. His blue eyes sharpened, and when he raked them over me, he looked eerily like his son. "She used black magic on me, just like *you* did when my son was only a boy!"

"It's not black magic," I protested. "It's—"

Tom pointed at me, his finger trembling. "You traumatised him, making that hole appear right in front of him—a hole that almost sucked him in! After that, he became unmanageable, always in trouble. To this day, I can't keep control of him."

"It was an accident, and it didn't have anything to do with how your son turned out."

"No." His head snapped up. "I don't believe that. You were a freakish child out to get my son, and years later you and your mother are still using your witchcraft!"

I started to tell him that Mom wasn't in a position to use magic anymore, but the wind took the words right out of my mouth. It rose around us, sharp and biting, and at the same time, the sky turned a shade darker.

"Did you see that?" Nick shouted over the roar of the wind.

Before I could answer, a brushing noise battered the landscape. It sounded like the bristles of a toothbrush swishing over tile, only magnified about a hundred times. I exchanged a startled look with Nick.

"What the hell's going on?" Luke demanded.

The wind settled down. The odd noise stopped for a brief moment, but then picked up again, loud and insistent. It seemed to come from everywhere all at once. I peered up at the sky, now a dusky grey. A chill swept me from head to toe, but it had nothing to do with the wintry air.

Nick clutched my hand. "What is it, Julia?"

No, it can't be. But there wasn't any other explanation as to why darkness was descending at record speed.

"I think…" I said, licking my dry lips. "I think they're painting over the mural."

Chapter Twelve

I wasn't sure what was louder now — the sound of my heart trying to beat its way out of my chest or the jarring noise that surrounded us, brushing, scraping, closing in from all sides.

"What is this?" Tom asked. "More of your black magic?"

"No." I glanced up at the golden hue of twilight filtering through the trees. "*They're* painting it over. The city."

"How can you be sure?" Nick asked.

"It has to be! Why else is it getting dark in the morning?"

There was another lull in the swishing. Nick leaned against me. "We have to get out *now*," I told him. "I need to open the portal before there's nothing left of the mural."

He squeezed my hand. "You got this."

This time I closed my eyes by choice and let my mind fill with thoughts of Mom. I wondered how things might've been different if she'd still been wearing the locket during the fire. Her Vista power wouldn't have been activated, and she might have made it out in time. At times I missed her so much I felt sick to my stomach. I pushed that feeling to the forefront now, allowing my deep sadness to overshadow everything else. My breath hitched, and one by one, tears leaked from my closed eyes and slid down my cold cheeks. There were no sobs, no wailing as I cried—just a quiet outpouring of grief and regret.

I waited for the dizziness to hit, expected my eyes to seal shut.

But neither of those things happened.

I opened my eyes. Nick was watching me with concern. Luke let out a grunt of impatience, while his father eyed me with suspicion.

And there was no portal.

"What happened?" Nick asked. "When you cried yesterday that glowy thing appeared."

"It didn't this time? You didn't see anything at all?"

"Nothing."

"What's the deal, Princess? Get us out of here."

My teeth clenched. "I'm trying, Luke. I don't know what's going on. Maybe too much of the mural is gone already."

Luke balled his hands into fists at his sides. "Try again, dammit."

Tom gave a bitter laugh. "If you came in here to help save me, Lucas, this is a pretty pathetic rescue attempt."

Luke ignored him. "Just get me and my father out of here."

I let out a shaky breath. "I'm doing what I can, okay?"

Nick ran his hands down my arms. "Hey, it's—"

He didn't get to finish the sentence because Tom talked over him, glowering at his son. "It's your trust fund, isn't it? That's why you want me back so badly."

"Trust fund?" Nick echoed.

"His grandmother left it to him when she died, with instructions that he receive it when he turns eighteen, which is next month. The catch is he only gets it after I sign it over. So he's not here for me. He just wants to make sure he gets my signature."

Suddenly it all made sense — how Luke desperately wanted his father to get his memories back, how he kept threatening me to get them home. That greedy, vengeful prick wanted his inheritance.

"It's worth a half a million dollars. He'd do anything to get his hands on that money. Believe me... That's all he's after. He doesn't give a damn about me."

Luke rolled his eyes. "Oh, give me a break. Don't pretend like you're Father of the Year. You were too busy getting drunk to pay attention to me."

"I would've done anything for you, Lucas, but you've always made things so difficult for me!" Tom jabbed a finger in my direction. "Ever since you exposed him to magic, he's been a troublemaker. That hole did something to him that day. I just know it."

"I told you," I said, swallowing my anger, "it was an accident." I shot an uneasy glance at the sky. For the moment, it was still that same shade of grey, and the brushing sound had stopped. But I knew it could start up again at any second. It was only a matter of time before more paint was rolled on the wall and we'd be goners.

"Just shut up, old man, and let Julia do her hocus pocus."

I turned to see Luke take out his lighter and box of cigarettes again. "Do you have to do that *now*?"

"Yeah, I do," Luke said, lighting up.

"Wait a second." Nick took a step towards Luke. "Let me see your lighter."

Luke narrowed his eyes as he took a long drag. "Why?"

"Come on, man. I just need to look at it."

"That's his memory trigger," I said. "He can't give it to you."

"That's not what I'm asking," Nick replied, his gaze trained on Luke. "Just hold it up for a second."

Luke grumbled but held the lighter out with a mocking flourish. After a few seconds, he slipped it in his pocket. "Satisfied? It's just a damn lighter."

As he'd stared at the silver object, a faraway look had come into Nick's eyes. Now he shook himself a little, as if coming back to the present. "I recognise it. I remember those initials."

I laid a hand on his arm. "Did he have the lighter with him the day of the fire?"

Nick pursed his lips like he did when he was trying to solve a complicated math problem. Then he put his hands to his temples and closed his eyes as if he had a headache.

After a moment, he opened his eyes and focused on Luke again. "The day you came to Julia's house, I was lying there, in and out of consciousness. But now I remember hearing you ask Charlotte where she sent your dad."

"Wait a minute," I said. "He was still asking about Tom when my house was burning down?"

"No, I don't think there was any smoke at that point."

"But then, why were you unconscious *before* the fire broke out? Luke said you breathed in smoke and — "

Luke puffed on his cigarette. "Who cares about those pesky details?"

"*I* care," I said. "What did you do to him that day?"

Luke held up his hands. "Hey, I didn't do anything. It's not my fault if he hit his head on the table when I pushed him out of my way."

I let out a shuddering breath, for the moment forgetting all about the clock that was ticking closer towards our deaths. "You knocked him out? You told me he was unconscious because of the smoke!"

Luke shrugged, flicking his half-smoked cigarette on the ground. "It was a busy day. I can't keep it all straight."

"That's not all he lied about," Nick continued, his voice quaking with anger. "When I came to, he was waving that lighter around, threatening to burn something if Charlotte didn't go get his dad."

I whirled on Luke, my heart in my throat. "It was you. *You* started the fire."

Tom gasped. "Is that true, Lucas?"

Luke ignored his father and flashed me a chilling smile. "I'd like to see you prove it, Princess."

"Tell us what really happened, you asshole." Nick's hands shook as he took another step closer to Luke. "Or we can arrange to leave you here."

"You're just trying to pin the fire on me because you couldn't protect your girlfriend's mother."

Nick's face turned beet red and his eyes darkened. A warning light went off in my head. I knew that look.

"Nick," I said sharply, "this is not the time. Don't do anything you'll regret."

Ignoring me completely, he hurled himself at Luke.

Luke lifted his forearm in one quick move and easily deflected the punch. But Nick followed up with a swift knee to his groin.

Luke's face crumpled in pain. He bent over, his hands covering the injured area. He spluttered, his breath coming in wheezy gasps.

"You son of a bitch," Nick said, panting. "Charlotte died because of you, didn't she? You— You're psychotic."

Luke staggered to his feet. Even as he struggled to draw breath, he flashed Nick a vicious smile. "Well, maybe it's true what my old man said. Maybe Julia here made me that way."

Nick rushed at Luke again. This time his fist made solid contact. Luke flew backwards with the force of the hit. He landed on his butt in the snow, rubbing his cheek. It didn't take long for the dazed expression on his face to turn into one of utter contempt.

"This is the last time you get in my way, Loverboy."

He jumped to his feet just as Nick reached him. They lunged for each other, grappling and twisting. Nick managed to land a punch in Luke's stomach. He dragged him to the ground, where he straddled him, raining blows on his head as Luke fought for breath. Then the two of them were rolling and grunting, fists flying. At some point, Luke gained the upper hand, launching a series of punches to Nick's face. Nick fought back, but I could tell he was losing energy as Luke, bigger and faster, overpowered him with a force that terrified me.

"Stop it!" I shrieked.

Tom, who'd been watching the fight in shock, suddenly sprang to life. "That's enough, Lucas!" But

Luke didn't slow, even though Nick was barely moving now.

"I said, break it up!" Tom threw his body in between Luke and Nick, which was the stupidest thing he could've done, because the second he did, Luke's fist connected with his jaw. He swore and fell to his knees.

"Oh, for God's sake," I said.

A medley of emotions flowed through me — anger towards Luke, fear for Nick's life and an overwhelming sense of panic at the out-of-control situation. It wound through my insides until I felt like I was choking. Sobs clawed at my throat.

No. You haven't come this far just to lose him all over again.

I rushed at Luke from behind, flinging myself on his back.

"What the hell…?" He tried to throw me off, but I twisted one of my hands in the collar of his leather jacket, grabbed a handful of hair in the other and pulled as hard as I could.

Luke howled and stumbled through the snow away from Nick, with me still clinging to his back. My stomach gave a lurch as he spun me around wildly, trying to shake me off. His feet hit a patch of ice and he pitched forward onto the ground, taking me with him. Together we slid down a small slope. When we stopped, I extricated myself from him and scrambled to my feet.

"You bastard. What is *wrong* with you?"

He curled his mouth in disgust. "What are you talking about? Your boyfriend attacked *me*! Pretty shitty timing since we're supposed to be getting out of here."

As if on cue, the brushing sound resumed and the earth quivered beneath my feet.

Then the grey sky darkened to a shade of midnight blue.

I took one step up the slope, desperate to see if Nick was okay.

But Luke clutched my arm, stopping me. "You're wasting time. Open the damn portal and get me out of here!"

"I don't have to do anything!" The scraping was louder now, more insistent, but I yelled over it, straining my vocal cords until my throat burned. "I can leave you here to die, just like you let my mom die!" Fresh tears filled my eyes. "Nick and Tom can go home, but not *you*."

Raw anger stung my body. The world began to tilt on its side. I closed my eyes and pictured Tom and Nick on the grassy area across from the mural. After a few breathless moments, I opened my eyes again.

Once again, there was no hole in the mural. There was no way out.

Then I saw it.

A narrow shaft of light filtered through the darkness. It was faint but steady, laying a golden hue over the snow beyond the slope. And as I hurried up the hill, I caught a glimpse of Nick and Tom captured in its whirlwind, their bodies a blur. A second later the portal swallowed them whole.

Even after they'd gone through, the doorway to home remained open. I ran towards it, Luke at my heels.

The ground started shaking. I lost my balance, teetering in the snow as the mountain vibrated around me. I slammed into a tree, scrabbling at the bark for a hold. And my heart skipped a beat because in the spot where I'd just stood, the ground split open, creating a gap about six feet wide. The portal stood open on the other side, unreachable, its light dimming with each passing second. The vortex, already weakened substantially, was not strong enough to pull me in from this far away.

The shaking stopped. The shuffling abated. I stared down at the chasm in the earth.

In the sudden silence, Luke called out from behind me. "What's going on? It's not enough that we're being painted over in here, but now there's a fucking earthquake?"

Aunt Karen's words came back me, about the force of opening a portal. It was amplifying the tremors that I assumed were caused by the weight of the paint roller. "I think the portal's causing it."

"Well, how do we get in there?"

I turned. Luke's dark shape was bearing down on me. "We'll have to go around," I said. "Just be careful. The ground's not stable."

But before we could move, the ground started to shake again. Luke stumbled backwards. The scraping had morphed into a horrific crashing sound. Luke cried out as he was tossed in the vibrations. I held onto the tree with all my might.

The quaking stopped once again. A hush fell over the mountain.

"Luke?"

No answer.

Damn it, what was I waiting for? The bastard could stay. I had to get out.

"Julia!"

It was the desperate tone that gave me pause, made me take a few tentative steps in that direction. The crack was now about ten feet wide.

"Julia, down here!"

He'd tumbled into the gap, somehow managing to grab onto a ledge jutting out from within it. I knelt at the place where his fingers curled over his tenuous handhold. He looked up at me with pleading eyes.

"Help me up!"

I hesitated. He was responsible for the fire and, ultimately, Mom's death. He was a monster who didn't give a damn about anybody but himself.

I glanced at the dying portal. By this time, it'd shrunk to an opening about three feet wide. If I crawled around the gap in the earth, maybe I could still get through it. I could save myself, while leaving Luke to his demise as the mural crumbled around him. I'd leave him, just as I'd said I would. I didn't care that he'd claimed to know some secret about eliminating the Vista magic. It had to be a lie, just like most everything else that came out of his mouth.

"You have to help me," he grunted, purple veins popping out on his neck as he struggled to maintain his hold. "I'm sorry about your mom. It was an accident, I swear. I just meant to scare her a little so she'd bring my father back. But she tried to knock the lighter out of my hand and I fell against the curtains. They caught on fire."

Hot tears stung my eyes and my heart broke all over again. Mom was gone because of a stupid kid with a lighter.

The rumbling resumed, bowling me off my feet. Chunks of rock began to rain down. A few of them glanced off my head, making me cry out. The ground heaved and fell in all around me, new cracks opening up. I lifted my head. Luke's hands were slipping.

The world that was my mural began to spin like a Tilt-A-Whirl. Fear struck me like a blow to the stomach — fear that I wouldn't get home alive, fear that I'd never see Nick again. Mixed with this fear was a flood of love and relief. If I were going to die, at least I'd die knowing Nick had made it home safely. He was alive, and that was all that mattered.

With my emotions rolling through me in waves, my eyes were glued shut. When I was able to open them again, I sobbed with relief.

Because I'd breathed new life into the portal.

A shimmering door now reached to the tops of the fir trees and stretched as far as the eye could see. It burned as bright as a thousand suns melted together as one. I squinted into the light and what I saw took my breath away. There *was* a sun on the other side, an autumn sun whose rays touched maple trees bursting with red and gold.

They paled in comparison to the colours of my painting, but they were real and true. They were the colours of home.

Then the vortex was back, reaching out for me.

"Julia!" Luke screamed.

I glanced down at him and caught a glimpse of the terror stamped on his face. And just like that, I decided. No matter what he'd done, no matter what lies he'd told, his death wouldn't be on my hands.

Just as the whirlwind enveloped me, I leaned down into the crevasse and grabbed Luke's hand. He found purchase on the rock face with his other hand and clambered up beside me, panting.

And we were pulled into the portal together.

Time stood still for me as we made the journey.

The crashing and shaking faded. I moved up and away, captured in a mind-numbing spiral as the last traces of the mural were obliterated. As I rode the wave, a vision of Nick came to me. He was waiting for me across from the wall, his crooked smile soft and tender. He was my end goal. He was home for me.

With this thought, the ride became smoother, slower. A balmy autumn breeze lifted my hair and caressed my cheek. A low whistling sound drifted towards me. I landed softly, sinking onto the bench, right on target. I opened my eyes.

Luke was slumped on the bench next to me, semi-conscious. A thin stream of blood oozed from a deep gash in his head where a rock had struck him.

"Julia?"

I turned in the direction of the voice. Nick sat on a patch of grass to the right of the bench. Tom stood a few feet away, pacing, but he stopped when he saw us and descended on Luke.

Nick struggled to get to his feet, but I was already launching myself at him. "Thank God you're all right!"

I threw my arms around his neck. He gathered me into his chest and I melted against him. But when he winced, I eased back. "*Are* you all right?"

As I studied his facial injuries, something yanked at my heartstrings. His right eye was swollen half shut and puffed out in a disturbing shade of purplish-black. Deep red welts marked his cheeks, and his nose sat at an odd angle. Blood caked his lips.

"Actually," he said with a little smile, "I feel like I've been clobbered with a baseball bat."

"Don't worry. You got in a few good hits of your own."

He let out a choked laugh. "Oh, good to know."

I ran my hands up and down his arms. "At least you're in one piece. When I saw you lying on the ground, not moving, I thought I'd lost you all over again."

"Nah. You're not getting rid of me that easily." He caught one of my hands and squeezed, and his voice dropped to a whisper. "I was so scared you weren't going to make it out in time."

"I didn't think I was going to. The portal was closing fast and... I don't know. It was like with the mural starting to disappear, even my worst emotions weren't enough to make the opening bigger."

"So what happened?"

"I thought of you, and the portal got about as big as a football field." I touched his cheek. "A Vista's power is triggered by strong emotions. Love is pretty damn strong."

He closed his eyes and pressed his forehead to mine. My head tingled in response.

When we drew apart, I murmured, "I could've left Luke in there. After everything he did, I was so mad. And I was going to. But—"

"But what?" he prompted.

I glanced over at the bench, where Tom was speaking quietly to his son. "I just couldn't do it."

"Turns out you didn't have it in you, huh?" He gave me an affectionate nudge. "I'm not surprised. You're nothing like him, Jules."

The whistling I'd heard on the way down grew louder. We all turned towards the mural—or what was left of it. A man stood at the wall, whistling, paint roller in hand, in the process of covering up the snowy village with a thick coat of grey. He wore headphones and was so intent on his task that he had neither heard nor seen our arrival. I wondered how he could've missed seeing the portal open. Maybe with the paint rapidly covering up the mural, it hadn't been visible from this side.

My gaze swept over the mural, and my breath caught in my throat. The mountains were almost painted over. Talk about cutting it close.

"I'm fine, old man. Just give me some space!"

I exchanged a look with Nick. Obviously, Luke was fully conscious again.

"You're not fine. You need medical attention."

"So does Nick." I dug in my pocket and pulled out my cell phone, which had miraculously survived the journey in and out of the village. "I'm calling Aunt Karen. She'll pick us all up and take us to the hospital."

"No way," Tom said. "We're not going anywhere with you witches. Let's go, Luke. We'll walk."

Nick shook his head. "Come on, man. He's bleeding and probably needs stitches. You can't walk to the hospital."

"We can and we will." Tom's eyes were cold and hard as they fixed on me. "God knows what effect your witchcraft is going to have on my son this time."

Nick got to his feet with a grunt. "Excuse me? Who was it that went in there after us? Who worked her butt off to save us? You wouldn't be standing there if it weren't for Julia."

"I can expose her for what she really is, you know. She'll be locked up for life."

"Oh really?" Nick said, folding his arms over his chest. "And what would you say to people? That there's a girl who can open doors into paintings? You really think anyone is going to believe that? You start going around telling everyone stuff like that and you'll be the one thrown in a padded cell."

Luke, who'd been strangely silent, pushed to his feet with a sigh. "Just forget it, old man. This is a waste of time."

"Maybe for you, Lucas, but I'm the one who's had to watch his son throw his life away after a little witch —"

"Or maybe," I broke in, "*maybe* you just needed someone to blame for Luke's personality and bad choices. Or here's an even crazier idea. Maybe your drinking was part of the problem. It was easier for you to blame Luke's behaviour on me than to take responsibility and be a real father."

For a second, my words seemed to hit home. Something like regret passed over Tom's eyes. But it was gone as suddenly as it appeared, and the look of scorn returned to his face. "Don't you tell me how to parent."

"And you know what else?" I continued, my voice harder now. "You should be grateful that I don't turn Luke in for arson."

"Or send him through another portal," Nick added. "Actually, if you ever bother either of us again, she will."

At that, Tom's mouth opened and closed like a fish. Then he shook his head. "Come on, Lucas. We're out of here."

Luke took a step after his father, who was already hurrying down the street. Then he stopped and turned back to me. He cleared his throat, hesitating. "Listen... I *am* sorry about your mom. I never meant for it to go down like that."

I nodded. At least he sounded half-genuine for once.

"And...thanks," he said in a gruff voice, "for helping me get through the portal."

"Is it true?" Nick asked. "You wanted your dad back for his signature?"

Luke shrugged. "Well, yeah. With that trust fund, I can do whatever I want. I can move far away from him and never have to deal with the bugger again."

"Good," Nick said. "And we won't have to deal with you again, either."

"The feeling's mutual, man."

I narrowed my eyes at Luke. "You lied about what happened on the day of the fire. Did you also lie about knowing a secret about my magic, about how to get rid of it?"

"Actually, that part was true." He paused. "After your mom explained what she'd done to my dad, she told me she was hoping to stop the magic. She said she was investigating Frank Marsten."

"The head judge for the mural contest?" I said. "What does he have to do with anything?"

"Your mom found out that Marsten's ancestor — a great, great, great-grandmother or something — was responsible for starting your freaky magic in the first place. He put a curse on one of *your* ancestors so that every firstborn child down the line would open paintings if they had a meltdown." He shrugged. "Don't know why, though."

My knees turned to Jell-O, and when I spoke, my voice was hoarse. "Marsten is the one who changed the day for the mural to be painted over. Originally it wasn't supposed to happen until next week."

Luke dabbed at the cut on his head, grimacing. "Well, your mom thought Marsten also carried on his family's magic. She was convinced he could reverse the curse."

"But how did she find any of this out?" I asked. "And why did she tell you about it?"

"Sorry, Princess. That's all she said." His cheeks flushed. "I was getting impatient by that point and all I wanted to know was how she was going to get my old man back."

In other words, that's when he'd started waving around the lighter and threatening Mom.

"But, for what it's worth," he continued, "I hope you get some answers." Luke turned to follow his father but stopped and glanced back over his shoulder, curving his lips in a wicked smile. "Oh, and just a friendly warning. You might want to drop the whole aspiring artist thing. It worked out better for Bob Ross than it ever will for you."

* * * *

Ten minutes after I called Aunt Karen, her Corolla pulled up in front of us with a screech of tires. She flew out of the car, and before I could say a word, caught me up in a bear hug, sobbing. "Oh, thank God you're okay."

Good. She's relieved.

Then she held me at arm's length, her forehead furrowed as she sniffled. "I nearly had a heart attack when I got your text. I told you to wait for me!"

And also pissed.

"There wasn't time," I said. "Jennifer called to say the mural was going to be painted over in the next couple of days." I bit my lip, still reeling from the news that Marsten might know how to take my magic away.

"I couldn't wait for you. If Nick and Tom were alive, I had to try to find them."

Aunt Karen turned to Nick, her hand flying to her mouth. "She found you. We thought you were…"

"Dead," he finished. "Yeah, I know."

She squeezed his hand. "We're glad to have you back. I can't imagine what you've been through. What happened? You look like you've been in a fight."

"Luke happened," I said with a tight smile. "It was his lighter that started the fire."

She drew in a breath. "What? How?"

"It's a long story, but here's the *SparkNotes* version." I briefly filled her in.

"What about Tom? You didn't find him?"

"Oh, I found him. He already left with Luke."

Her eyes widened. "You just let them go?

"What was I supposed to do, Aunt Karen? Turn Luke in for arson? Like the police would believe me. No one saw him that night. He snuck out through the backyard."

She pursed her lips. "I'm just worried. What if Luke's father comes after you again?"

"Somehow, I don't think that's going to be a problem," Nick said, putting his arm around me.

* * * *

That evening I sat on the edge of my bed, staring down at Nick. He was tucked under my comforter, sound asleep.

It was hard to believe that just that morning I'd watched, terrified, as Luke had pinned him to the ground, hitting him over and over again. Sighing, I smoothed a strand of hair off his forehead.

At least he looked a little better now, with the dried blood washed off and his broken nose realigned. The ER doctor had advised him to take over-the-counter pain relievers and apply ice to his face to help the swelling go down.

When we'd gotten home from the hospital, I'd urged Nick to take a nap in my bed. He hadn't argued.

Aunt Karen had coaxed me to lie down in her bed and get some rest, too. I couldn't think about sleeping yet, though. I was too wired. Too much had happened in the past few days, too much to process. And maybe it sounded crazy, but I didn't want to be apart from Nick. I'd just gotten him back. I wasn't ready to let him go just yet.

There was a light knock on the door frame. "Julia?"

Aunt Karen stood in the doorway, frowning. "I thought you were going to sleep."

"No," I said in a low voice. "I can't."

She massaged her forehead, but the lines only deepened. "Then come downstairs and have a cup of tea with me."

I hesitated, glancing back down at Nick.

"He'll be fine. He's not going anywhere, okay? And I really would like to talk."

I eased myself off the bed. "I guess I can take a few minutes."

"I'll go put the kettle on."

As soon as I heard her footsteps going down the stairs, I leaned over Nick. "Don't worry," I whispered, lightly tracing his jawline with my finger. He stirred but remained in a deep sleep. "I won't be gone long."

Down in the kitchen, my aunt was arranging cookies on a plate. Her hands shook a little. "Aunt Karen? You all right?"

She jumped, startled. "Yes, of course." She turned her back to me to open the fridge but not before I noticed the glimmer of tears in her eyes.

"Hey." I crossed the room and put a hand on her arm. "What is it?"

Her shoulders sagged. "Nothing. I just... I was so worried, Julia. When you went in there, I had no idea what was going to happen or if I would ever see you again."

"I know," I said, hugging her. "It was pretty scary."

"I told the school you had to go away for a family emergency, and Roxy's been pumping me for details. All I could tell her was that it was a personal matter and I didn't know when you'd be back."

Roxy. How in the world was I going to explain all this to her?

The kettle whistled, and she wiped her eyes. "Now let's have some tea. It's like I always say, a hot beverage makes everything better."

I stared at her. Now it was her turn to look at me with concern.

"What?" she asked. "What did I say?"

"There was a woman in the mural. Her name was Susan. She reminded me of you. Then there was this real bitch, Stacey." I shook my head as I got two mugs down from the cupboard. "She was a lot like Trisha from school. It made me wonder if I was thinking about people from my life when I painted these characters."

"It makes sense. You poured so much of your heart and soul into that mural. I can't imagine what it must've been like, seeing it come to life like that." She peered at me. "What exactly happened in there, Julia?"

She listened in shock as I told her the story — minus some of the more private moments with Nick — over cups of hot tea. When I finished, she leaned back in her chair and drew a long breath. "Restoring memories through touch? That's incredible."

"Yeah. Good thing we figured it out, too. After losing the picture, I didn't know what I was going to do."

She took a sip of her tea. "And all along, Luke wanted his father back so he could sign over his trust fund? I'm sure there must be a stipulation in place where if Tom disappeared or pre-deceased him, he could still get the money. Eventually."

"Yeah, the key word there being 'eventually'. Luke is too impatient to wait for red tape like that." I tapped my nails against the ceramic mug. "You know, his relationship with his dad is so messed up. Our family isn't what you'd called 'normal', with the whole witch thing. We have our secrets, and Mom hid *a lot* from me. And I was so mad at that. I still am, in a way. But then I saw how Luke and Tom were with each other." I gave a little shudder. "And it made me think that no matter what she hid from me, at least Mom and I had a good relationship. I have a lot of happy memories, you know?"

She squeezed my hand. "I do know."

I paused. "There was something else Mom hid from us." I explained what Luke had told me about Marsten and the Vista curse.

"How in the world did she find that out?"

"That's what I'd like to know. I think I'm going to do a little digging into the Marsten family."

"Julia…" Her forehead was creased with concern.

"Don't tell me you don't want me to look into them. I *have* to know, Aunt Karen."

"No, it's not that. I'm all for finding out a way to end of the curse. It's just… I want you to be careful while you're looking. You can't let anyone know about your powers. You saw what happened when Tom and Luke Mercer found out."

She had a point. But I had no intention of broadcasting my abilities to the world, now or ever. "Believe me," I said, "I don't want anyone else to know about them, either."

"That includes your friends."

Before I could respond, the doorbell rang.

"Expecting someone?" I asked.

She shook her head and rose. "I'll get rid of whoever it is."

A minute later, Roxy's voice drifted down from the foyer. I leapt up from the table and rushed into the hallway.

"And she's not ready to —"

"Roxy?" I interrupted my aunt's excuses. When my best friend saw me, her face broke into a huge smile. She held a plain white envelope in her hand.

"Jules! There you are. What's going on? Are you okay?"

"I had to go away for a few days, but yeah, I'm okay."

"Good. I wasn't sure if you'd be here or not but…"

Aunt Karen cleared her throat. "And I was just telling her you weren't up to having company. It's been a long day for you."

"No, I'm fine. Really." I gave my aunt a pointed look, hoping she'd clue in to the fact that I had no intention of spilling the beans about my powers.

"I can't stay long anyway," Roxy said. "Mom needs the car to go to her Pilates class."

"Well, all right then. I'll leave you girls to it."

As soon as my aunt disappeared up the stairs, I pulled Roxy into the living room. She laughed as we fell together on the sofa. I slung an arm around her. "You're a sight for sore eyes, Rox."

"What's going on, Jules? Your aunt acted like you were on some top-secret mission. I couldn't get anything out of her."

I bit my lip. "Well, it's a long story, but…" I took a deep breath. "I went to find Nick."

She stared at me. "Nick."

"Yeah. Um, I know it sounds insane, but he's alive. He didn't die in the fire."

"*What*?" She gripped my hand. "What are you talking about? Where is he?"

"Upstairs."

Her eyes, round as saucers, roamed over my face. "Are you serious?"

"Completely. Turns out he…well, he got out of the fire alive, but he kind of had amnesia."

"You're pulling my leg."

"No, I swear. It's the truth."

She didn't say anything for a long moment. A myriad of expressions crossed her face. Disbelief. Confusion. Shock. "How did that happen? Where has he been all this time?"

"I'll explain everything when we have more time." Before I saw her next, I'd have to come up with some kind of cover story. "The main thing is that he's okay and he remembers everything now."

She let out a relieved breath. "Well, thank God for that. When can I—?" Her cell phone rang, cutting off her question. "Hang on. Hello? Yes, Mom. Okay. I know. I'll be there soon." She tossed the phone back in her bag. "Ugh! Sharing a car with Mom is a pain in the ass. She needs me home ASAP. Sorry, Jules. I want to hear *everything*, though." She clutched my arm again, her nails digging in. "This is unreal. I can't believe Nick is alive. After all you went through, you must be going crazy with relief."

"Yeah." I smiled. "I guess I am."

"Oh, I almost forgot." She picked up the envelope she'd set down beside her. "This was sticking out of your mailbox when I got here just now."

I took the envelope from her, frowning at my name printed in sloppy letters on the front. Inside I found a small white box. I lifted the lid.

My locket lay in a tangle in the bottom of the box. The silver heart caught the light streaming through the window. I felt the locket calling out to me. It wanted me to wear it.

"Who's it from?" Roxy's voice broke through my reverie.

I put the lid back on the box, effectively stifling the locket's voice, then dipped my hand in the envelope again and pulled out a folded piece of paper. My heart gave a lurch as I scanned the note.

"Well?" Roxy prompted.

I stuffed the paper in my pocket. "It's from Tara, one of the student aids in the school office. Someone turned the locket in."

Roxy wrinkled her nose. "Weird that she just left it in the mailbox without calling or anything."

I shrugged. "Yeah."

"Well, I'm glad you got it back it, Jules. I know how much it means to you." She peered at me. "Aren't you going to put it on?"

"Of course. Um, I just want to show Aunt Karen first."

She threw her arms around me with a giggle. "What a crazy day. You've got your locket back, Nick's back... I can't believe I have to go before getting to hear the whole story!" She got to her feet. "Amnesia? Sounds like something from a cheesy movie."

I forced a laugh as I walked with her to the door. "I know, right?"

After I closed the door behind her, I pulled out the note and reread it.

Julia,

I found this on the floor outside history class the day of that lively discussion about freaky magic in the mines. I held on to it, planning to pawn it. Then I realized it was yours. I couldn't let you have it back until my old man was out of the mural, kind of like insurance that you wouldn't lock away those magical emotions of yours while I needed them. Anyway, now you can control your magic until you get the curse undone. Of course, this will mean you'll go back to being the 'Ice Princess', but I figure you won't mind too much.

Luke

I clutched the box in my other hand so tightly that my fingers hurt. I should've known Luke had stolen my necklace. But he was wrong. I *did* mind going back to being the Ice Princess. I minded a lot.

I went upstairs to my bedroom and stopped short in the doorway. A pair of caramel-brown eyes watched me from my bed.

"Hey there, stranger," he said.

"Hey, yourself. How are you feeling?"

"Better. Though I'm pretty sure I look like I've been in a bar room brawl. Did I hear the doorbell?"

"Yeah, Roxy stopped by. I told her you were here, but she doesn't know the whole story. Aunt Karen thinks we should keep it a secret. And, as much as it's going to suck to hide this from my best friend, I think she's right. The fewer people who know, the better."

"Then we won't tell my parents, either."

"What *will* we tell them?"

"That I hit my head on my way out of the fire and lost my memory. Then I wandered around until my memory came back."

I rubbed my forehead. "You think they'll buy it?"

"I don't know. But at least it's partly true." He flashed me a grin. "And the best thing about amnesia is that I can say I don't remember how it all went down. So, we can be fuzzy on the details."

I smiled back. "You're a pretty smart guy, Nicholas Allen."

"Hey, I didn't lose all my brain cells while I was trapped in your painting." He nodded at the box in my hand. "What's that?"

"My locket. Apparently, Luke found it. He left it in the mailbox."

"Oh my God, that's great!" He swung his legs over the side of the bed, his grin widening. "You can control your power again."

I set the box on top of my dresser and wiped my sweaty palms on my jeans. "Yeah, I guess."

His smile dimmed. "What's wrong? Why aren't you happy about getting it back?"

Heaving a sigh, I came to sit down beside him. "I am. I mean, it's all I really have left of Mom. And if I wear it, my emotions will be in total control all the time. I know how important that is, to keep my power at bay. It's just… I don't want to rely on a charm to do it."

He nodded. "You want to find out if Marsten really can take the magic away."

"Yeah, I do. He might be a psycho who wanted to keep you and Tom trapped in the mural for some reason, but I have to find out if there's a way to get rid of this power. I don't want to pass this on to my firstborn."

"Yeah, I get that."

"And in the meantime, I want to control my emotions myself, so I don't have to be totally numb anymore. If I could find a balance, you know, like let myself feel some things without going into total freakout mode. Do you think that's possible?"

He smoothed his hand over my hair. I leaned against him. His touch had a calming effect. "I do. But you don't have to make a decision right now, Jules. The important thing is you have it. If you need it, if you do find yourself having a meltdown, it's there. You have the option."

"That's true," I said softly.

Nick cleared his throat. "Not to change the subject, but I'd really like to get in touch with my parents now. You said you have their new number, right, Jules?"

Sitting up straight, I gazed at him intently. The evening sun seeped through the window behind him, its golden rays moving through the glossy folds of his dark hair. It was something I never thought I'd experience again. "Are you sure you're ready?" I asked, pushing down a rush of emotion. "We can wait until the morning."

"No." He shook his head. "I'd like to see them."

"Do you want Aunt Karen to call them? She could invite them to come over."

"Yeah. Yeah, that'd be good."

I gave his hand a reassuring squeeze. "Everything's going to be okay."

"I know. You're right. It's just that..." He let out a weak laugh. "For some reason I'm nervous about seeing them."

"Don't be. They'll be freaked out, but in the end, they're just going to be happy to have you back."

* * * *

We were in the kitchen when the doorbell rang about thirty minutes later. Nick shot me a nervous look across the table. "This is it," he said.

"I'll go," Aunt Karen said, pushing her chair back. "You kids wait here."

We listened to her footsteps as she walked down the hallway to the front door, and a moment later, muffled voices when she let in Mr. and Mrs. Allen. Nick took a deep breath and stood just as his parents appeared in the kitchen doorway.

Mrs. Allen took one look at her son and her face crumpled. "Nick?"

"Yeah, it's me, Mom." Nick turned to give his father a shaky smile. "Hi, Dad." For his part, Mr. Allen stood with his mouth agape, blinking as if he couldn't believe his eyes.

Nick's mother rushed over to him, tears sliding down her flushed cheeks. "Karen told me that you were here, but I didn't believe it." She patted his arms and shoulders frantically, as if trying to assure herself that he was real. "I don't understand. How is this possible?

We thought you—" She broke off as her voice caught on a sob.

"We thought you were dead," Mr. Allen finished for her. He remained rooted to one spot on the floor, unable to take his eyes away from his son.

"No," Nick said softly. "I made it out of the fire."

"Oh, thank God. Thank God." Mrs. Allen threw her arms around him. A lump rose in my throat as I watched.

Finally, she drew back, her red-rimmed eyes moving across his swollen face. "Are you okay? What happened? Have you been in a fight?"

"Nick and Julia will tell you the whole story," Aunt Karen said, as Mr. Allen took his turn to grip his son in a tight embrace. "Why don't we sit in the living room where it's more comfortable? I'll make coffee."

In the living room, Nick's parents sat on either side of him on the couch, their eyes scarcely leaving his face for a second. Aunt Karen and I took the chairs opposite.

"I feel like I'm dreaming," Mrs. Allen said. "I just can't believe you're here."

"Where have you been the last two months?" Nick's father asked.

I exchanged a look with Nick. Then we began to tell his parents our cover story. As Nick had suggested, we kept the details sparse, ending with the lie that when Nick's memory finally returned—*after* he got in a fight, meaning the details were fuzzy on that too—he called his parents' old phone number. When he found out it was disconnected, he then called me and I picked him up.

By the time we'd finished recounting the concocted story, Mrs. Allen's face was pale and drawn. Mr. Allen clung so tightly to his coffee mug his knuckles turned white. They'd been quiet as they listened, both of them wiping away what seemed to be an endless supply of tears.

"Amnesia," Mrs. Allen said in a dazed voice. "I just can't get over it."

Mr. Allen shook his head. "This does feels like a dream. A damn good dream."

After setting her mug down on the coffee table, Nick's mother crossed the room to me. Startled, I put my own mug down just as she enveloped me in a bear hug. "Thank you for picking him up. We're so grateful. Thank you," she repeated in a whisper. "We're so happy to have him back. We thought we'd lost him."

"So did I." As Mrs. Allen released me, tears pricked my eyes. I dashed them away with my hand before they could gather any momentum and swallowed the lump in my throat. A deep breath helped settle the swirl of emotions — relief, pride, happiness and sadness that Mom wasn't here with us.

And as those feelings settled, safely under control again, I made a decision.

* * * *

Sometime later, I found myself alone in the living room with Nick. Mr. Allen had excused himself to make a call and Aunt Karen and Mrs. Allen were in the kitchen making more coffee.

I'd joined Nick on the couch, and as I leaned my head on his shoulder, my thoughts turned to the mural.

The snowy village remained imprinted on my brain. I could still see every detail in my mind — the lines and colours, the shapes and contours. I closed my eyes, and I could still feel the blustery wind on my face, hear the crunch of snow beneath my feet, smell the firs dancing on the mountains. But they were just memories. The mural was gone. So was Mom.

Nick knuckles brushed my cheek. "Hey," he said softly. "You okay?"

I opened my eyes. "Yeah, I was just thinking about the village. It's really gone now, isn't it?"

"Yeah, I think it is." He put his arm around me. His touch helped warm the cold ache in my chest.

We were both silent for a moment, lost in our own thoughts. Then I lifted my head and asked, "So what do we do now?"

"We move forward together. It's what your mom would've wanted."

As he enfolded me in a comforting embrace, I held on tight. In the midst of all that seemed surreal, he was my anchor. He was solid and real.

I pulled away with a smile. "You okay here? I need to go upstairs for a sec. Be right back."

"Sure."

Back in my room again, I picked up the box. I ran my fingers over the lid but didn't take it off. I knew that if I did and caught sight of the locket inside, the pull of the charm would be too strong for me to resist. Instead I strode purposefully to my closet and tucked the box far back on the top shelf. Then I stepped back with a satisfied nod.

After the fire, I'd been numb. And at the time, I'd been okay with that. I thought things were better that way. But now, having gotten a taste of what it was like to really feel... I wasn't sure if I could ever go back to being the Ice Princess, to being closed in by that wall of numbness. I knew if I worked at it, I could experience emotions and keep my magic in check at the same time.

I'd done it just moments before while listening to Nick's mother, and I could do it again.

Hopefully, I wouldn't have to struggle with that balance for long. I'd find out if Marsten really was the key to reversing my power, and maybe, before long, the Vista magic would be eliminated…forever.

Confident in my decision, I went back downstairs. Nick looked up as I entered the living room. His crooked smile sent butterflies skittering through my stomach.

When I reached out for him, I didn't feel numb.

I felt alive.

Want to see more like this? Here's a taster for you to enjoy!

Demigoddess 101
Kacie Ji

Excerpt

I know it sounds ridiculous, but from all the hoopla I've heard about birthdays, I half expect just once to be greeted by a chorus of angels singing me into this new era of my life. You know, something special. Something just for me. But the logical side of me knows that I'll open my eyes and see nothing more than the same old blush pink that has clung to my walls since my 'I'm a pretty pink princess' kick when I was five.

Just like I do every year.

Of course, my logic wins out and I'm greeted by the cheery, if fading, pink. As soon as my eyes become accustomed to the retina-searing combination of wall and jovial brilliance of the morning sunlight, the reality sets in. Having a birthday during final exam season has proved that I'm not destined for anything special. This year I have two final exams on what should be a glorious day. So instead of a day gallivanting in the sun celebrating, I'm stuck slaving over a standardized test that will prove nothing more than my ability to regurgitate facts.

Fun.

With a sigh and a stretch, I get out of bed and stare out at the world. I know what I'm going to see. A couple of oak trees, the street, maybe a glimpse of the sky if the wind is blowing the branches and their accessorizing foliage just right.

This morning I notice a scarf dangling from the second oak. I have to admit I'm a bit confused as I watch it twisting and turning, dancing in an unseen breeze. It's not like I routinely go around decorating my trees with frills. It would be nice in the winter, I suppose—it would give the trees a little life—but I digress.

I stare at it a moment. It's plain, but pretty. Someone out there has to be missing it. Pushing open my window, I stare at it a moment then reach out for the gauzy material only to find that it's caught on a gnarled branch. I pull on it gently, afraid to tear the fine material. After all, it'll be mine if no one comes to claim it. I lean out a little to try to untangle it. The wind plays with me for a few seconds before I finally manage to snag a gossamer edge with my fingers again. I give it a couple of experimental tugs, releasing it in shock when it yanks back.

"What the—?"

Must be the wind playing with the branches.

I shimmy out farther, determined not to let a stupid scarf outwit me. Reaching out once more, I wind a length of it securely around my wrist so it doesn't get away from me. I wrench again. This time it jerks back violently, and I could swear that I saw a hand do it.

I let go, heart throbbing in my ears. Did I almost just yank someone out of the tree?

"Sorry! Is someone up there?"

The scarf flows upward like a silken waterfall in reverse and disappears into the dense layering of leaves. Well, that answers my question. Then it occurs to my slowly waking brain that there might be someone camping outside my window in my tree. The scarf couldn't belong to a peeping Tom... I don't think. Unless a floaty silk scarf has become an accoutrement for *en vogue* stalkers these days.

So this fashion diva in my tree doesn't seem like so much of a threat. However, there is still the issue of their being stuck in my tree.

"Um, are you okay up there? Can I get you a ladder or something? Someone to shoot you out of my tree, maybe?"

"Ava, dear! Time to get up!" My mother, Tess Goddard.

She's always been loud, which was good since I always had advance warning before she made an appearance — an Advanced Mother Warning System. I bet other kids wish they were so lucky. The sing-song voice comes from the other side of the door a second before my mother sweeps in.

A lot of people have told me that we could almost be sisters — almost. I don't know whether to take offense or not. I mean, to be told that you almost look like a sibling to a woman who's in her mid-forties isn't exactly something a teen girl wants to hear. But it always brings a glow to Mom's face, so I guess it's worth the perceived insult.

Although, when I look at her, I can understand how she could be seen as younger. Her ebony hair is still as glossy, thick and dark as ever. And her stormy gray eyes, so like mine, are vibrant and brimming with life. So looking at her is like looking in a mirror — if it aged you about twenty-five years.

Right now, the aged version of me has dragged me from the window and wrapped her arms around me for a bear hug. The woman may be small, but she's got the grip of an anaconda.

"Happy birthday, Ava darling! Eighteen! It seems like yesterday I was in agony for forty-six hours trying to bring you into the world, and here you are now, a gorgeous young lady."

I go through this every year. The hug and the weepy speech. Though this time she seems weepier than usual. I let her manhandle me for a little while longer. It only seems fair to suffer this for a few minutes annually when she went through nearly two days of agony. Only a few more to go before the debt is wiped clean, by my count.

Finally, she sniffles and relinquishes my person, restlessly smoothing my hair and patting my shoulders and cheeks like she can't get over what she's seeing. "My baby is eighteen. I cannot believe it."

I try my best at a gentle smile. Any wider and she'd think I was mocking her, too small and I would be accused of faking. "If you're going to keep this up, I'm not going to make it to my finals."

"Oh!" She hugs me again, this time releasing me after a second. "I'm being silly, of course. But it's not every day a daughter—but I'm babbling again." She pecks my cheeks and rocks back to smile at me. "Get dressed. You have a big day ahead of you."

"Mom…"

Too late. She's gone. Never mind. It's probably best that I don't tell her. At least not until I find out if there really is someone out there. Let's hope that if there is a person up in my tree that they are a trapped supermodel and not a serial killer. I can't help but giggle at the insane thought. The scarf probably got blown up there on its own and I just imagined everything else.

But just to make sure, I lean out of the window once again to try to see if I can spot a person in it. "Hey! Someone up there?"

No reply and I can't see anyone. The tree's leafy, but not that leafy. I'm pretty sure that I'd be able to spot anybody in it. I can't see the scarf anymore either. Damn it! That was a nice scarf.

Shoving disappointment aside, I start on my morning routine. Seeing as it's a nice, warm spring day, I throw on a simple T-shirt with my favorite pair of jeans. I pull my hair back in a ponytail, slip on my black strappy sandals, apply makeup with a light hand and I'm good to go. All this was done in the bathroom, of course. Just a precaution until I find out whether or not there is really someone in my tree.

My bag is heavy with the books and notes I packed the night before. Textbooks I have to return, notes to cram before the test, all the things every girl wants to think about on her birthday.

What does surprise me, though, is the spread my mom has on the kitchen table. We're not especially morning eaters. I might have a piece of toast and some juice, maybe cereal if I'm feeling crazy, but nothing too heavy before noon. What is laid out before me is amazing, seeing as Mom hardly ever cooks. Quite frankly, I'm not even sure she knows how to work the stove.

Belgian waffles complete with cream and fresh fruit piled high is the centerpiece of the meal. A fruit salad, glasses of milk, juice and water are also present, arranged in an artful way — if you can arrange drinks in an artful way, that is. I don't think I've ever seen any meal in this house with this much thought and care put into it.

"This is amazing! Thank you!" I throw my arms around her and give her a big wet one on the cheek. It's the least I can do for all this, even if the thought of eating all that makes me want to get in front of the TV and play *Just Dance* for the next two days. But being the dutiful daughter that I am, I plunk myself onto the chair and dig in.

I manage to get everything down and get up just as I see Mom ready with a second helping. I feel like an overblown blimp as it is. Another mouthful and I'd explode for sure. Or at least burst out of my clothes. Images of me doing my exams in the nude quirk my lips for a second. Um, yeah. Not going to happen.

I wipe my mouth with an intricately folded napkin and get up. "I've got to run! I have some last-minute cramming to do." I peck her cheek again. "Thanks. I'll see you later."

I manage to somehow make it out through the door without keeling over. I'm surprised I can even walk after eating all that. Leaning against the banister, I take a moment to breathe, hoping that it'll settle. It takes more than a few heaving breaths to convince my stomach to retain what it's holding. I lower my head back in an attempt to try to stop reverse peristalsis. That's when I notice the oak tree again.

All gastric-related discomfort is now forgotten as I take a look to see if my Peeping Tom fashionista is still up there.

A furtive glance around me lets me know that I'm all alone. "Hey! You still up there?"

No answer.

"I want you gone by the time I get back, all right? I'll call the cops if I see you again." There. The threat of getting the law involved should be enough to scare them off. I mean, how would they survive in jail if they can't leave their couture at home while stalking?

Proud of myself, I saunter off to academic hell.

Sign up for our newsletter and find out about all our romance book releases, eBook sales and promotions, sneak peeks and FREE romance books!

About the Author

Ann Miller writes young adult novels about first loves, family secrets, and magic. She grew up in Nova Scotia, Canada, where the local bookmobile fed her diet of Nancy Drew mysteries, Sweet Valley High books, and Stephen King horror. After graduating from the University of King's College, she moved to Newfoundland, an island that makes up for its unforgiving climate with beautiful coastlines and majestic icebergs.

When she's not reading or writing, Ann can be found spending time with her husband and son, or binge watching Netflix while curled up with the two four-legged members of her family.

Captured in Paint is her first novel, and she has several more in the works. You can take a look at Ann's website and follow her on Facebook and Twitter

Ann loves to hear from readers. You can find her contact information, website details and author profile page at https://www.finch-books.com